To Pam, who continues to help me

become who I might be.

Perry and the Big Hustle
(Blotch Book Three)

By Stuart E. Schadt

Bradley Stuart Books
U. S. A.

Perry and the Big Hustle
(Blotch Book Three)
By Stuart E. Schadt
Copyright ©2018 Stuart E. Schadt
All rights reserved.
Published by Bradley Stuart Books.

Printed in the United States of America.

ISBN 978-0-9907610-6-8

First Edition

Friday Night at the Banners

On Friday nights Shannon's parents, the Banners, make Shannon and her two brothers stay home for dinner and family time until nine. They invite friends. It is a lot of fun, and the food is always great. I wanted to go, but my grandparents were in town to celebrate my birthday on Saturday. When you're an only grandchild, you get a lot of attention. Remember Gramps remarried and his wife Candace has two other grandchildren, but they are older. Gramps and Candace are staying at the Choice Inn. Pop and Nanna are staying at our house. They arrived while I was in school, and the garage has been off limits to me since they got here. Someone even papered over the windows. Does that mean I'm getting a car for my birthday?

The reason I wanted to go to the Banners was that they were all going out to eat. The topic on these first nights of visits was always about how I was being raised, and I was sure there would be a lot of discussion about the night I didn't come home and how my parents handled it. I think this is due to how young my parents were when I was born. Maybe back then my parents did need more help and support, but as far as I was concerned, we were doing okay on our own now.

I was so thankful when they decided to let me go out with my friends. Dad drove me to pick up Cam and then to the Banners. On the way to Cam's, he asked, "Do you know the difference between sex and love?"

I turned red, "This will go easier if you just tell me."

"In this story, *Tales of the Mountain Boy*, the father tells his son sex is like a two-piece puzzle. It easily fits together. Actually, it fits together a couple of different ways."

"Dad?! (I'm not sure whether that gets an exclamation point or a question mark, so I gave it both.) Move on to love."

"Love is like a ten thousand piece puzzle where you don't even have the picture to go by, and at times it's difficult, and at times it's easy, and it's amazingly rewarding the longer you work at it."

I told him, "I like that. Dad, I promise after I can drive myself, we will still talk." We were at Cam's, and I went up to the door to get her. She was ready.

Since it was my birthday weekend, she agreed to sit in the back seat with me, but she sat way over by the door. She told Dad, "I always have to be on my guard; your son can hardly control himself in my presence."

Dad smiled, "I do see the untamed animal in him." Dad looked up in the mirror so I could see his eyes, he was smiling.

I defended myself, "I have my different drives and motivations well under control, and I am in no way dangerous."

Cam said, "Mr. Larcon he should be featured on that show, 'Dangerous Predators.'"

Dad agreed, "I'll send in his picture."

I was so glad when we pulled up at the Banners. As we walked to the door, I kept making a low growling noise and leaning toward Cam's neck. She laughed and pushed me away, "See that only proves what I was saying."

Shannon answered the door. We went in and joined the party.

I walked up to Josh and gave him a long hard hug, and I whispered in his ear, "Happy Birthday brother." He whispered the same back to me. He isn't really my brother.

Rick who was standing nearby said to Cam and Shannon, "Sorry girls, I guess they're joining my team."

Josh reached out and touched his arm, "Oh, Rick, if I were switching teams, you'd be the first person I'd call."

Rick turned bright red, and everyone laughed.

There was El Salvadoran food, which uses mostly the same ingredients as Mexican food, but in different ways. I ate more than my share.

Josh and I had said no presents, but there were presents. Josh got mostly revolutionary war soldiers, which he wanted because he uses them as models to improve the graphics in the war game video he is making. He also got some comic books.

The Banners gave me a laminated card that said, 'Free pass to the Banner's hall bathroom.' Everyone laughed at that. Sean got me a Shenandoah National Park knife. As I showed it around, he announced, "Cam told me that was a special place for you." I turned bright red. Cam laughed embarrassingly loud. Everyone shouted, "Tell."

As straight-faced as I could be, I said, "Well I was only there once as far as I know." Cam laughed again, and everyone else shouted, "Tell," again.

Cam said, "Oh man up and tell them."

I looked at this wonderful group of friends, "Well if you ever came to my house for dinner, I'm sure my parents would tell you. It's where I was conceived."

Trent, Shannon's older brother, said, "Oh dude that is so unbelievable. Does anybody else know where they were conceived?"

Everyone else said no.

Rick asked, "Your parents don't really tell that story to just anyone do they."

I told them, "Mom told it to Cam the first day they met."

Rick mumbled, "That is some weird stuff."

I said, "Tell me about it. My mother ends the story with, 'there was a smell of honeysuckle in the air,' and I want to crawl under the table."

Cam handed me her present. I could tell it was a jar. When I unwrapped it, I turned bright red. It was a jar candle, fragrance honeysuckle. She said, "You told them, I didn't."

Josh gave me a key to his house. I gave him a card that said, 'One free trip to the CVS drugstore.' He turned bright red, but we both refused to explain it. I also got additions to my Sponge Bob, Little Pony, and Scooby Doo comic collection. (This is a joke Josh started.)

We gave Josh a ride home. He sat up front with Dad, I rode in the back with Cam who sat right beside me. We took Cam home first. (Dad's decision.) I walked her to the door. I told her, "This was the best birthday ever."

We kissed. I'm sure you're tired of hearing it, but I still get an amazing feeling all over my body when we kiss. As we separated she said, "Your birthday isn't over yet. See you tomorrow." And she disappeared into the house.

At Josh's, I got out to get up front. Josh said, "You don't need to walk me to the door, but can we hug again," and we did.

When we pulled apart, he wiped a tear from his eye. I asked, "What's up?"

He said, "Having you for a brother is the best thing that ever happened to me." And he left.

In the car, Dad asked, "How was the party?"

I told him, "Dad, I love having friends."

Do I Bear the Mark of Cain?

People were still awake when I got home, but they were heading to bed. I watched videos on my computer for a while. I knew he wouldn't see it until morning, but before I went to sleep, I texted Josh, 'Love you brother.'

I drank three ice teas at the Banner's, and around two I woke up needing to pee. When I finished, I decided to go peek in the garage. Instead of a car for my birthday, I found Pop's Jeep. They seemed to be playing some cruel prank on me. Remember, Dad and I talked about how they would hide my Christmas present and leave clues to lead me to it. Maybe this was like that. Anyway, no car dreams tonight.

I woke at eight. While my computer powered up, I checked my phone. Josh had written back at three, 'Love you brother.' I bet he had to get up and pee also. I went to my computer to check my email. I don't like to look at them on the phone because typing back is so hard. Josh calls me an old man whenever I say this. There were some birthday greetings then one with no name,

'Blotch = Mark of Cain'

I knew this was something biblical. I went right to Wikipedia. Cain killed his brother Abel, and God banished him and marked him. No one knew exactly what the mark was. What did this mean? I never had a brother until I found Josh, and he's not really my brother. I deleted the email.

Dad, Pops, Gramps and I headed over to Burgers and Billiards at eleven thirty. We were having lunch and playing pool. We weren't due home until two. The cool thing was that three times strangers came over to have their picture taken with me. I'm still famous from Blotch vs. the Canary. That was when I set this guy in a yellow shirt up and wagered my pool cue against five hundred dollars. I went home with my cue and five hundred dollars.

We got an audience when Gramps and Pops put up fifty each, betting I couldn't clear the whole table without one miss. I had to take out all the stripes, then all the solids and then the eight ball. I stayed focused, but I think as the crowd grew, there were a lot of side bets. I did it just fine. I got the two fifties from Pops and Gramps, but a bunch of other people just threw money on the table while I was putting away my pool cue.

I told them, "See it's like I'm a street performer. People give me money to watch me play or to watch me beat them."

Gramps said, "It still looks a lot like hustling."

Before we left, Mr. Jakes, the manager, came over, "You know kid you sure are great for business. I wish you would come around more often."

I said, "I wish I could, but I have school and stuff."

Speaking of school, I realize I don't talk about it much. It's really kind of easy and doesn't cause me a lot of stress. I know it annoys Josh how I spend half as much time studying as he does, but he says it makes him glad because it makes me available for math tutoring. In return, he looks over my reports and essays before I hand them in. He's a great proofreader. He catches things spell check seems to miss, and also I always confuse homonyms, and he catches them. Sometimes, he tells me my argument is weak, or my meaning is unclear. I have to fix that myself.

When we got home, I went to my room. More birthday emails, texts and another:

'Blotch = Mark of Cain.'

I emailed Josh, 'Look up Mark of Cain, talk tomorrow.' I was sleeping over at Josh's Sunday night because my grandparents would all leave Sunday afternoon, and Josh had an Algebra test Monday morning he wanted me to help him prep for.

Cam and her parents came over at four. The weather was nice, in the high seventies, so we were doing burgers on the grill in the backyard. Cam's parents hadn't met Gramps and Candace, so we did all the introductions.

We had burgers and cake. Cam cut me a corner piece and then shoved it in my mouth and all over my face. I guess I'll never learn. I do love that girl. Pop's got it all on film. After cake, Dad brought out a piñata shaped like Sponge Bob.

I laughed, "What is that? Am I getting candy for my birthday?"

Cam said, "No, but the birthday boy gets to break open the piñata. Stand up and come here." Mom handed her a blindfold, and she tied it on me. Dad was holding a stick with the piñata attached to a string. Cam spun me around.

"Am I facing the piñata?"

Cam said, "Yes, tap it with your stick."

I tapped it. I reared back and swung with all my might. I hit nothing but air and lost my balance stumbling forward. Everyone laughed. Dad said, "Take off the blindfold." I did, and he held the piñata in place while I went to town on it. As it broke apart, no candy came out. I saw nothing drop but tattered shreds of Sponge Bob. Dad said, "There's something there look for it."

I pulled keys out of Sponge Bob's leg, "These are the keys to Pop's Jeep."

Pop said, "No, I don't think so."

I held them up, "Yes, this is your keychain with the star on it."

He said, "Not anymore."

"What are you telling me?"

He laughed, "Nanna and I are downsizing to one car. I'm giving you the Jeep."

"Really? Really? This isn't some bad joke?" I turned to Dad, "Is this okay? Can I have it?"

He said, "There are some conditions, but yes you can have it."

I was so excited I didn't know what to say. In Virginia, there is no driving test if you pass Drivers ED, but you have to go to court with a parent where a judge talks to you about the responsibilities of driving. Josh and I were scheduled for court at four on Tuesday, April ninth our actual birthday. I couldn't wait. With all the excitement of the party over, Cam and I went to my room. We kissed, and we even laid down beside each other on my bed. (We're not supposed to, but I was sure we would hear anyone coming upstairs. And I'll confess it's not the first time we broke that rule.) I told her, "I think I'm the luckiest boy."

She was looking right at my face, "Your face just fell, what's wrong?"

I said, "What do you mean my face fell?"

"You said you were lucky, but then you thought of a reason you weren't lucky. You better not be sick again. I'm tired of you always ending up in the hospital near death. It's exhausting." She was overly dramatic. The lying down mood was over, and we were sitting up.

I told her, "I've been getting these disturbing emails. I've gotten two." I turned to my computer, "Look I got another, 'Blotch = Mark of Cain.'"

Cam asked, "Are you planning to kill Josh? Because even though sometimes I'm jealous of how much time you two spend together, I still like him."

"No, I'm not going to kill Josh, and I didn't know you were jealous."

She said, "Just a little, but I asked my parents if you and I could have a sleepover and they said no, so I guess there isn't much I can do about it."

That made me smile, "So what do you think this is?"

She said, "I think it is someone messing with you. Don't let it get under your skin."

I was sitting on my desk chair, and she was sitting on my lap. We did some more kissing.

Sunday Morning

First thing, I went out to wash and clean the Jeep, but Pop had it so clean, there was really no point, so I just sat in it and listened to the radio. I am so lucky. Pop came out at ten, and we went for a drive. He gave me an orientation to the vehicle, you know, where the lights turn on and the wipers and the flashers and all that. He showed me there's even a special toolkit for taking off the doors and the top. When we got back, we went in to talk to Dad about the conditions.

Dad was very serious, "I wanted you to have to work for your car so you would value it, but Pop wanted to do this, and it makes sense. The Jeep is totally yours, but the right to drive is a privilege and a responsibility. Do you understand?"

I said, "Yes sir." Remember I made my parents agree that things given to me are mine, but I understood how this was different.

Dad went on, "Gramps is going to pay your insurance and two tanks of gas a month for six months, but after that I expect you to be earning enough to pay your own way."

Before everyone left, I did all I could to tell everyone how much I appreciated them coming for my birthday and for my presents.

Dad and I went over to Josh's at six. We took the Jeep, and I was driving. Dad said, "I guess this really is the last time, we do this. There are probably a lot of things I should still tell you, and I hope I get to tell you, but there is one thing I want to make sure I say in case we never get to talk again."

I was stopped in Josh's driveway, "Wow, Dad, quite a buildup."

He got out because he was taking the Jeep home. I got out and grabbed my book bag off of the back seat. Dad came around and gave me a big hug and said, "Son I love you, and I'm proud of who you are becoming."

Out of a stunned stupor, I replied with a weak, "Thanks, Dad." He got in the Jeep and left.

I knocked on the door but when no one answered, I let myself in with the key Josh had given me for my birthday. I knew they might not be back yet, from their afternoon movie. I went and lay down on my bed in Josh's room. It was a real bed. I had stayed at Josh's for a week once when my parents wouldn't let me come home, and since then I had an inflatable bed in Josh's room. They had gotten me a real bed for my birthday. Between the bed and what had happened in the driveway, I was overwhelmed. I was certain my parents and the Bentons couldn't love me as much as they did if I had killed a brother.

After a while, I rallied and got out Josh's algebra book to look at what we needed to go over. He had left some notes on the things he thought he really needed help on. Top of the list was, 'everything.' In reality, there were four things, and I thought we could work on each one for twenty minutes with five-minute breaks between each block. We would work for fifteen minutes and then I would have him tell me what we had just done without looking through the material. This is how you make studying work.

I was back lying on the bed reading the newest issue of Defenders when he showed up. I gave him a few minutes to unwind. He had eaten junk at the movies, and I had a late lunch so we would have a snack later. I put him to work. He's gotten better since I've been working with him. Each of our study blocks tonight only took fifteen minutes, so with breaks, we were done in little over an hour.

We headed to the kitchen. Josh's parents were in the den watching TV. I walked over to Mrs. Benton and leaned down and kissed her on the cheek. When I rose up, I said, "Thanks for my bed." I went over and shook Mr. Benton's hand. Mrs. Benton said, "I already cleaned the kitchen. You boys don't make a mess."

I guess to defend her kitchen from the hoard of two teenage boys, she followed us. She pulled a container out of the frig, "Here are two leftover pork chops you can microwave. How does that sound?"

I said, "Sounds good to me." Josh agreed. We headed back to his room with our pork chops. Yes, with plates and napkins.

Josh said, "So did you have a brother? Maybe you shot him when you were little."

"Josh, we don't have any guns."

Josh said, "Maybe that's why. Let's check birth records and see if you had a brother. I still have my aunt's passwords for Ancestor Search." He typed in some stuff. "You're showing up but no one else, so no brother."

I laid back on the bed, "So who's sending this. Why are they messing with me?"

"If you pull up your email, I can copy the header and find out if it's local and where it was sent from."

I pulled up my email, "Don't open any of those Cam sent me, just the Mark of Cain one."

"Is she sending you pictures?" I blushed. He asked, "Are you blushing because she is or because you wish she would?"

I rolled over and buried my face in my pillow. He laughed. I had barely recovered when he said, "Okay, they're coming from computers in the school library."

I went and looked over his shoulder, "You are brilliant."

He said, "This is elementary stuff; You could probably do it. You start by searching, 'How do you trace an email?' and follow the steps."

"Thanks for the vote of confidence. So, someone at school is trolling me. I don't get it. And using Blotch. I don't get it. How did they send them on Saturday?"

He turned from his desk, "Duh, timed sending! He/she goes in on Friday writes and sends with a time delay because they think they're hiding their tracks. Why don't you ask your parents what it means?"

I was sitting up on the bed, I laid back dramatically. "We only just recovered from my whole 'Blotch Drama.' I'm not sure I can stand to start a new one. Anyway, there's no harm coming from this."

He was going to call Shannon, so I texted Cam, 'Want to go for a walk?'

Back from her, 'Too cold come over.'

I whispered to Josh I'd be back by nine, put on my coat and headed to Cam's. Mr. and Mrs. Benton were in the den as I headed out, I told them, "Cam invited me over."

Mrs. Benton said, "Be home by nine."

I said, "Will do."

At Cam's, Mrs. Grant let me in and sent me up to Cam's room, I said, "Door open."

She said, "Good boy."

Cam hugged and then kissed me as soon as I walked in. When we separated, she asked, "Is Josh ready for his test."

I sat on her bed, "Not to brag but his math grades are up a point and a half since I've been tutoring him. We found out the 'Cain' emails are coming from a computer in the school library."

She sat beside me, "Let it go. Don't let this get to you."

"I'm not, I promise. I won't obsess over it." She is right I have gotten overly focused on things at times, and she worries about me. I decided not to mention it again as Josh, and I continued to hunt the guy down.

She reached under her bed and got out a wrapped present. "Here's something for your birthday."

I unwrapped it, "It's a purple steering wheel cover, your favorite color."

She smiled, "You're right! Purple is my favorite colors, but that's a coincidence. I just thought it was right for you."

I kissed her, "You are so funny. Now, whenever I'm driving, I'll be thinking of you."

She said, "I like that."

I was home at Josh's by nine, and we were in bed by ten. I know there are kids at school who push themselves to stay up late. If I wasn't here, Josh might stay up another hour or two playing some online game, but I like to sleep, and one of my tutoring conditions is that especially before a test, he has to be in bed, lights out by ten.

"Goodnight Josh."

"Goodnight Bossy."

"Goodnight Moon."

Oh That Car Door

Josh and I walked into the cafeteria together on Monday. Everyone at our table got silent as we came near. Josh went and sat with his girlfriend, Shannon, he asked, "Are you talking about us?"

I sat across the table from Cam, because she still thinks I can't control myself if I sit next to her. She said, "You two think it's all about you, but it's not."

I was glad, "I don't want to be the center of attention."

Rick was laughing, "You don't like being the center of attention? A few months ago the whole school waited on the front lawn to find out if you were dead or alive."

I told them, "At the time I didn't think about it because I too was waiting to find out if there would be a happy ending, but mostly they stayed because they were blocked in by the wreck. So yes I get a lot of attention, but really I'm an introvert, and I find it exhausting."

Cam said, "Oh poor you, I'm about to come over there and let you lean against my shoulder while I stroke your hair and tell you everything is going to be okay." I pulled a chair into place for her. She shook her head no.

Gene walked up. He was resting his right hand against his body and was holding an ice pack. Ashtyn ran to him, "What happened let me see? This is bad. Did you show the nurse?"

He said, "She gave me the ice pack. I can't get into the x-ray place until after school."

Sean asked, "So what happened?"

He sheepishly said, "I slammed it in the car door this morning." His lights said he was lying. Cam looked at me, and I gave her an eye arch to tell her he was lying. When I concentrate, I see people's essences as auras and strings of light around them.

Ashtyn was making over him and helping with his food. It looked so bad that it hurt me to look at it. Josh asked, "Did they give you any pain medicine?"

Gene said, "After five phone calls and a signed permission slip my mother faxed over, they gave me two ibuprofen, and they said if I accepted any medicine from another student we would both be expelled. If some accidentally falls on my tray, I won't ask any questions."

The conversation moved around a bit and then Darden, who Gene used to hang with, showed up followed by Janessa, his girlfriend. The left side of Darden's face was bruised, and his left eye was swollen shut. He was carrying a straw hat, like a stage prop. Everyone immediately could see the tension between Gene and him. Sean said, "I guess you got slammed in the same car door Gene did?" Nobody laughed, but it lightened the tension.

Darden said, "I come hat in hand to apologize." He looked at the hat, "A little lame I guess." Turning to face Ashtyn, he said, "Ashtyn, I happened to encounter Gene in the boy's restroom before classes this morning, and I said some very inappropriate and horrible things to him, about you and about you and him. I regret every word I said. I'm sorry I hope you will forgive me." Gene was about to speak, but Darden raised his hand to say he wasn't done. "I have nothing against you Ashtyn, I was mad at Gene because I missed him; he was my best friend. He quit being a jerk, and I didn't, so he cut me off. Janessa has now convinced me that I just need to not be a jerk, and maybe Gene will be my friend again. Maybe she will still be my girlfriend. I hope you will help."

Ashtyn had been a boy, but in January she came back to school as a girl. She and Gene had been dating for several months. She jumped up and kissed Darden, "Of course I'll help. Gene come here and give Darden a hug." Looking at his bruised hand, she added, "You can't shake hands."

Gene had gone from angry when Darden arrived, to neutral, to positive. They had an awkward hug. Gene said, "Let's go see the nurse and get you an ice pack."

Darden said, "She's never going to believe we both ran into car doors."

Gene said, "We'll convince her." They headed toward the door.

Janessa grabbed Ashtyn's hand, "Come on Ashtyn, they have such a bromance that we will have to constantly remind them we exist." They went off together giggling following the boys.

Whatever Darden had said was so awful neither he nor Gene ever told any of us. I couldn't imagine what words were so vile that they would raise up such violence and I was amazed that they could go from busting each other's bodies at 8 a.m. to hugging each other at lunch.

Cam said to me, "Well I guess you would never stand up for me like that?"

She was talking about my commitment to non-violence. I said, "First off, anyone who would insult you should be more afraid of you than of me." I paused.

Cam jumped in, "As I've told you before if you have a first, you need to have a second."

I shook my head, "Second, I do think if someone said something so horrible about you that it was unrepeatable, I might be moved to violence."

That made her smile.

I Need a Job

During the afternoon I texted Henry, the student in the entrepreneur's program who manages the coffee shop and asked if I could come talk to him about a job. He wrote back, 'Come after school today.'

At the coffee shop, I walked up to Henry who was behind the counter. He said, "Go have a seat at one of the tables; I'll be out in a minute."

I went and sat down. I wondered why he didn't give me an application to fill out while I waited? This was the first job interview I'd ever been on, so what did I know.

Henry came and sat down. Very formally he said, "How can I help you?"

I said, "I'd like a job."

"Why here?"

"I need car money."

"That's why you want a job, but why do you want to work here?"

I thought a minute, "I see the people behind the counter, and they seem to enjoy what they're doing. It looks like a good place to work. Will you consider me for a job?" I felt he was a bit cold in his treatment of me. We weren't friends, but we were acquaintances, and our mother's both worked for the library system.

He said, "Here is how it is, Perry. Many of the people I hire, this is their first job. They learn the responsibility of showing up when they are scheduled to work. They learn what is appropriate to wear to work and what is not. They learn the task of making coffee. 'I'd like a café grande, decaf, latte, low fat, lite foam, nutmeg, and cinnamon.' They learn to follow instructions. They learn to see what needs doing and do it. I estimate you could master all that on day one and there would be nothing more for you to learn. I won't hire you."

I asked, "Are you saying I'm too smart to work here?"

He leaned toward me, "I'm saying you came here because asking me for a job wasn't as scary as asking a stranger. I get that. I'm saying you need to find a job that will challenge you and teach you some things."

"Like where?"

He said, "I don't know. Maybe there is an atomic lab that needs someone to check their calculations."

I was bummed, "I guess you're right, but I still feel rejected and hurt."

He laughed, "I understand, but one of the posters in the Entrepreneur Lab says, 'If you can't overcome your defeats, you'll never try for your successes.'"

"What does that mean?"

He laughed again, "It means if you ask a girl out and she says no, you ask another girl out; if your first business venture fails, you don't quit. You try something else. If your first job interview doesn't land you a job, you go to a second interview. You don't give up."

I said, "Thanks."

He said, "Wait, don't go yet. Do you know what an elevator speech is?"

I said, "A speech to a small audience."

He laughed, "That's good. It's a short sales pitch, no longer than say a six-floor elevator ride."

"What am I selling?"

He smiled, "You're selling you. So here are the pieces: 1. Introduce yourself, name, a word about your family, best subject in school. 2. Why do you want to work at the particular place you are applying? 3. Close with some of your general attributes. You dress well, know how to speak appropriately with people, are always on time. Maybe how many hours you want to work a week."

I said, "Thanks," and left.

A few months ago, I would have thought Henry turned me down for the job because he didn't want his customers to have to look at Blotch, but now I honestly believe he thinks I need to seek a more challenging job to help me grow. I don't know why, but Henry is wise beyond his years.

I spent the last four months wrapped up in what Cam called my "self-created Blotch Drama." Since my parents signed the Emancipation of the Corpus of One Perry L. Larcon, which granted me the power over all medical procedures including the right to decide whether I kept or got rid of Blotch, I am fully committed to keeping Blotch. Blotch is the port wine birthmark on my left cheek, shaped like Michigan, upper and lower peninsulas. Pop and Cam finally got through to me that Blotch is an ability, an empowerment.

When I started high school, I started getting better about holding my head up and not hiding Blotch. However, I was doing it with an in-your-face attitude. I managed to change my attitude to say, 'Yes, I'm different, notice me.' The results have been amazing. I'll admit there have been a few reactions I felt were negative, but they don't bother me like they used too.

To lift my spirits, I called Josh as I walked home and told him about the interview.

Josh: Bummer. Do you think I'm dumb enough to work for Henry?

Me: I bet you are. Maybe you could drool during the interview so one of your learning goals would be to not drool into people's coffee.

Josh: I could learn not to fart in front of customers.

Me: Don't stir other people's coffee with your fingers.

We both laughed and went on for a while about learning goals.

Josh: We're pretty lucky to have girlfriends.

Me: What do you mean?

Josh: You're a math nerd. I'm a computer nerd, yet we have cute girlfriends.

Me: Speak for yourself in the nerd department.

Josh laughing: Whatever you need to tell yourself to sleep at night.

Is That Man Angry

Josh aced his Algebra test. He's on track to move up from C's to a low A. I take all the credit, but it's really the fact that he has put in the work, and I have helped him improve his study habits.

We went to court on Tuesday afternoon and got our licenses. Dad and Mr. Benton rode home together so that Josh and I could leave in the Jeep. At the very first red light we stopped at, a man walked in front of the Jeep and stopped. It was the Frisbee throwing man from the park. Remember I've seen him at the park three times throwing the Frisbee for his dog, and it ends up he's Marlin's dad, a kid on the spectrum I used to tutor. He looked mad, like furious. He made the sign for Perry, pointing at me with a 'u' and then touching the left side of his face and then his lips with an 'r' and then the sign for go. He walked on. A chill ran down my spine.

Josh asked, "What was that? Is that guy mad at you?"

I was shaking, the light turned green, and I headed to a parking lot. I had to get out and walk around. I came face to face with Josh, who had also gotten out of the Jeep. "Hey, tell me what happened. Who was that guy? What did all that mean? Why is he so angry? Why are you acting so weird?"

I couldn't process his overload of questions. I didn't know where to start. When I finally got it together, I told him, "I don't know why that got to me. Before I started school, I volunteered at a center for kids on the Autism/Asperger spectrum. I worked with two kids who are math geniuses. I just haven't been back. Cam and I ran into that guy in the park. He's the dad of one of the kids, and I told him I would go back. That was like a month ago, and I still haven't been back."

"What were all those motions?"

While doing the signs for U Blotch R, I told him, "He points with a U, then touches the side of his face where blotch would be, and then his lips with the sign for R. U Blotch R is the name in sign language that Marlin gave me.

Josh said, "Let's go now. It will get you in the door, and maybe you can set up a schedule. Do you need me to drive?"

"I think I do."

I gave him directions.

The center was in a one-story house that had been adapted for business use before the center moved in. We had to knock on the door to be let in. A woman answered who I didn't know, that threw me off. I had to introduce myself, "I'm Perry Larcon. I used to do math with Marlin and Pah. Is Mrs. Patel here?" The woman was still staring at me like I made no sense. I pointed at my chest, made the sign for 'u,' touched blotch, and touched my lips with the sign for 'r.' You might think I would use 'I' here, but it's not a statement. It's my name.

She smiled, "Come in. Mrs. Patel is out, but she'll be back shortly. Marlin asks about you often. Well less and less."

This was killing me. We walked to one of the back rooms. I could see Marlin, but his companion dog wasn't Sadie. "Where's Sadie?"

She put her fingers up to her lips, "Sh, he misses her more than he misses you. She died last fall, maybe late September early October."

I said, "No, I saw her in the park just a month ago with his dad."

She gave me a look and said, "Let's go back up front, so we don't disturb any of the kids, in fact, let's step outside."

Josh and I followed her outside, "Marlin doesn't have a dad. He has two moms. I'm beginning to feel uncomfortable about letting you in so I would appreciate it if you wouldn't mind waiting for Mrs. Patel here." She used her keys to let herself back in.

Josh said, "Are you in an episode of Twilight Zone or something? I mean, if you are, I'm glad to be along for the ride."

We sat on a bench on the front porch to wait for Mrs. Patel. We both started checking our phones.

When Mrs. Patel arrived, she was glad to see me, and I introduced Josh. I told her about my encounter with her assistant and with the man I thought was Marlin's dad. As I retold the story, I ended with, "But you know he never said he was Marlin's dad. I said it, and he didn't contradict me. Anyway, I'd like to come back and volunteer."

She said, "Perry, I'm so sorry, but the center is closing."

I almost screamed, "What, why, how, where will the kids go?"

She invited us to come in and sit in her office, "We're basically going bankrupt. The building needs fifteen thousand in repairs we don't have, mostly a new roof. Also, we didn't get a twenty-five thousand dollar block grant last year. I had really expected that grant, and I've been working at half salary. I can't do it any longer. The kids will go back into the public schools."

I abruptly stood up. I almost shouted, "No,"

She looked sad, "Perry, we have tapped out all our sources. I was at the bank today to see about a loan, but our only significant asset is the building, and we owe more on it than it's worth."

This was not going to happen. I felt my failure to volunteer had caused this. "How much time do I have?"

She was puzzled, "If you mean, when do we close? The answer is the end of May."

I was shaking, but I was strong, "So if I could get you forty thousand by the end of May, you're good."

She said, "Perry, the largest fundraiser we ever had only raised five thousand. We are just out; it's too late."

Josh and Mrs. Patel were staring at me like I was crazy. But a loud and condemning voice in my head was clearly saying, 'It would have been easier if you had come when you said you would.' I blurted out, "I know I'm late, I know, I get it, but I'm here now. Come on Josh." Turning to Mrs. Patel, I said, "I'll email you a plan by Thursday."

I headed for the Jeep. I gave Josh my phone and started the Jeep. "Text Henry. Use the Henry2 number. It's his private phone."

"Henry at the coffee shop?"

I said, "Yeah, he's the most business savvy person I know. Write, need to plan a fundraiser. Can we meet this evening? Perry."

Josh asked, "How do you have his number?"

I laughed, "I forget where I get stuff, but I don't forget numbers and addresses."

Josh said, "Here he is back, '7:30 @shop bring elevator speech. What is your cause? Why do you care? Why is it important? What do you want?' What's an elevator speech?"

I was turning into Josh's neighborhood, "You are supposed to be able to make your sales pitch in the time it takes to go six floors in an elevator. I'm going to ask Cam to go with me. Do you want to come?"

He said, "Since it's you, and I did so well in Algebra, I bet they let me. I'll text you if I can."

I let him out and headed home.

Forty Thousand Dollars?

Cam, Josh, Henry and I were sitting in a booth at the coffee shop. Henry said, "Pitch."

I started, "I volunteer at the Renaissance Center, a place for children on the Autism/Asperger spectrum. Particularly I work with Marlin and Pah, who are brilliant in math. A regular school with its rowdiness and noise would never serve them, but at the center, they excel. I am out to raise $40,000 for the center because without it they will close. I'm here to ask for your help in designing a fundraiser."

He looked at his watch, "Excellent, less than thirty seconds, so you could actually add additional information, maybe why the urgent need. Be prepared for how ongoing funding will be resolved. Okay, I'd like to walk you through and make you think, but I don't have time, so I'm just going to give you what I think you ought to do."

We nodded yes. We all had pads to take notes.

"First, you need a venue and a draw. Perry's fame as a pool shark is your draw, so Burgers and Billiards is a natural venue. Then, you need to identify multiple streams of revenue. Maybe the restaurant will give you ten percent of all tabs; you could have a silent auction; you get sponsors to give you monetary donations. Each level of sponsor gets different recognition. Finally, people pay to play Perry, and if they beat him, they get some sort of prize. Forty thousand is a lot of money." He paused for a moment, I imagined we looked overwhelmed; I felt overwhelmed. "This is doable, you need to break it down into pieces, and you need to ask for help. Right now I have to get back to work."

Cam was the first to speak, "We can do this."

Josh agreed, "I'm in."

I said, "I have to do this."

I took Josh home and then Cam. I told her, "I'm scared."

She touched Blotch, "Don't be scared. You just sleep on all this tonight, and tomorrow it will look as simple as a quadratic equation where x equals 40,000."

We kissed, for a while, and I headed home.

I did some reading and then went to sleep.

I had disturbing dreams in the night, but when I woke all I could remember was they involved the man in the park.

I looked at my phone after I dressed. Cam had texted, 'Dreamed it last night, we can do this.' I wouldn't see her until lunch.

She showed up to lunch with a ten-page business plan of what needed to happen. I was amazed. Ashtyn and Gene were going to handle sponsors. Josh had made an app to schedule reservations for seating at the restaurant. He needed to find out how many people the restaurant sat. I was to work on celebrity waiters, teachers, principals, people like that. There were still a lot of other jobs. Serena and Karalyne showed up from the mean girl table, both smiling.

Serena announced, "We're going to handle the silent auction. We'll get every store to contribute, mostly outfits but other stuff too."

Karalyne added, "Our goal is a hundred items priced between fifty and a hundred each. I guess you can do the math," and they walked away.

Josh said, "What just happened?"

I shook my head in confusion.

Shannon said, "They are just doing that so Karalyne can be close to Perry."

Josh said, "But how did they even know about it?"

Rick was looking at his phone, "Henry tweeted it out, along with a web page, a Fundsup page, and a volunteer's page. In addition to what we've talked about, he has an audiovisual team, a social media team, and a press and publicity team. He's named it The Big Hustle."

Sean asked, "Has the manager at B and B even agreed to this?"

I said, "I guess we'll head there right after school."

Cam and I were at B and B at four. Mr. Jakes said he could give us fifteen minutes. I gave him my improved elevator speech. I asked to use the restaurant as the venue and that we wanted ten percent of all the tabs.

He asked, "You think you can fill my restaurant from noon until six on a Saturday?"

Cam told him, "We plan to use reservations so we'll know going into it how we're doing."

He signed on, "Okay, I'm on board." We agreed to the third Saturday in May.

I went to the restroom before we left, Mr. Jake came back over to Cam, "Did your boyfriend ever call Mr. McDerman? The guy who owns the pool cue company wanted to talk to him after that video went viral. I bet he would at least give you something for the silent auction."

She said, "I don't think he did. He's had a rough year, he's been in the hospital three times. How do I reach him?" (This is one of those things I learned about later, but it's more interesting if I let you know now.)

Mr. Jakes told her, "The manager at the sporting goods store may have the info."

When I got back, Cam said, "Why don't you go on home, I want to do some girl shopping, I'll have my mother come get me."

I said, "Okay."

I kissed her and was walking away when she called out, "Don't forget to send the date and other info to Henry for posting and say thank you."

I blew her a kiss. She headed toward the sporting goods store.

Mom, Are You Mad at Me?

This year had put a lot of stress on our family and especially on my relationship with Mom so I've been doing things with her.

Two weeks ago I was with her, and we stopped at the grocery store. Previously, I would have stayed in the car and looked at my phone. Now, I went in with her. I asked why she bought one brand and not another, not about every item but, as we moved through the store, I engaged the process.

We got to the checkout line, and Mom realized she forgot the milk. I went back for it while she waited in line. By the milk cooler, there was a girl about three sitting in the shopping basket seat; her mother was also getting milk. The little girl pointed at my face and said, "Mommy, look at his face."

The woman turned and was horrified by her daughter pointing at me. I knelt down so that I would be eye level with the little girl, and said, "Hi sweetie."

She smiled, "My name is Bethany."

I said, "Hi Bethany, my name is Perry. This thing on my face," I turned so she could clearly see it, "Is a birthmark. I was born with it, I call it Blotch."

She said, "BoBo."

I said, "No, it's a blessing mark."

She spread her arms and made a kissing gesture, I looked at the mom, who nodded yes. I went in to kiss her cheek, but she pushed my face to the right and kissed Blotch. She said, "Blessing," as I moved away.

If this had happened three months ago, I would have left as soon as the little girl pointed at Blotch, milk or no milk.

I straightened up. The mom said, "Perry you are everything everyone says you are and maybe more."

I asked, "How do you know me?"

Offering me her hand she said, "I'm sorry, I'm Lisa Pennington. I work in the school district office, and I reviewed your application to take senior math. It came with a picture. My office also monitors students who leave school by ambulance. There have only been three of those this year, and two of them were you. Not to mention my husband loves pool, and he shows Blotch vs. The Canary to anyone who will watch it. Thank you for being so sweet to Bethany." The Canary was hustling kids out of their Christmas money playing pool. I hustled him back and took five hundred dollars from him. I'm a great pool player.

I told Bethany and Mrs. Pennington goodbye and left hoping Mom had not already checked out. She had, so I paid for the milk.

As part of my effort to rebuild our relationship, I try once a week to cook with Mom. I'm also learning how to cook, and I like it.

Tonight mom and I were making meatloaf together. She said, "Wash your hands, then put the meat in a bowl, add breadcrumbs, salt, pepper, and season salt. Then look in the fridge for something wet."

"What?"

She explained, "It needs more moisture. Maybe we have some barbecue sauce or some salad dressings but not one with oil, or you can use an egg."

In the fridge, "Here's some barbecue sauce, about a third of a bottle, here is also that Jamaican Jerk sauce."

She said, "Use all the barbeque sauce and just a spoon full of the Jerk sauce, it's pretty hot. Then use your hands to mix it all together." I started mixing the meat and stuff. "Mix it with more muscle, your acting like you're afraid of it."

I held up my hands with little pieces of meat clinging to them, "It's yucky. I feel like I'm working on a prop for a horror movie."

Very sharply she said, "Well you're not. You're working on dinner, get back to it."

I stared at her.

She turned away, "I'm sorry Perry I didn't mean that to sound so harsh. It does look like something from a monster movie."

I asked, "Mom, are you mad at me?"

She came over and touched my arm, "No, Perry maybe I'm just tired. I'll go rest while the meatloaf is in the oven."

When I had it mixed enough, I formed it into two loaves in the cooking dish and put it in the oven at three fifty.

"Mom, I haven't had a chance to tell you that after I got my license on Tuesday, I went and saw Mrs. Patel at the Renaissance Center."

This made her smile, "Oh I'm so glad, are you going to start volunteering again?"

"Well, I sort of volunteered to raise forty thousand dollars for her by the end of May. If I don't, she has to close."

I don't think I had ever literally seen anyone drop their jaw in amazement, but there stood Mom. "You what?"

I said, "I know it's crazy, but it's really happening, and people I don't even know are volunteering to help. Henry, Mrs. Miller's son at the coffee shop, named it the Big Hustle and already set up a website." I explained the overall plan to her.

"What about your school work?"

I said, "I've got that under control."

She said, "Well this brings up something your father and I have wanted to talk to you about. We can discuss it more at dinner."

We sat down to dinner at six thirty. I filled Dad in on the fundraiser. He was impressed by how much we had gotten done in just one day. I gave the credit to Henry for getting the website up and going. I brought up what Mom had said, "Mom said there is something you wanted to discuss with me."

Dad laid down his fork, "Perry, this is just a discussion. It's not a decision. It's a chance for everyone to share their thoughts. Do you understand what I'm saying?"

I said, "You're telling me I'm not going to like what you are going to say, but you don't want me flying off the handle, whatever that means. And by the way, your lights say that what you're about to say sucks."

Mom said, "I don't like that word, Perry."

I apologized, "I'm sorry. Go on, I'm ready."

Dad continued, "Perry, we don't think school is challenging you enough, and we are wondering if you should return to homeschooling."

I felt like Tristan had just punched me in the gut. I so totally lost my appetite that I thought about returning the food I had already eaten to my plate. I sat and looked at them. It was too much. I regurgitated all my dinner very quietly and neatly onto my plate. I covered it with my napkin looked at them, and asked, "Can I please be excused?" I got up without waiting for an answer, went to my bathroom, rinsed out my mouth and went to my room and quietly closed my door. I laid on my bed in total darkness.

After thirty minutes, I returned to the den, "I'm sorry. My reaction was involuntary. You're wrong because school is just as challenging as my homeschooling. I'm just using my free time differently. I now have friends. Things like this fundraiser will give me a chance to learn some new skills. I am getting pretty good at my elevator pitch. I asked Henry for a job at the coffee shop. He turned me down because he said there was nothing I could learn there, and I needed to find a more challenging job. He suggested there might be a nuclear lab where I could get a job checking their figures. I'm looking into that." They didn't think that was funny. "He did say that, and I repeated it to be funny, I guess it wasn't, but I am looking for a job where I will learn some things, and, if I can save the Renaissance Center, I'll return to tutoring there."

Mom said, "We appreciate you giving this some thought. If you are going to stay in public school, maybe there are some things you could do to up the challenge level. Perry, you are really bright, and we don't want you becoming mediocre."

Staying calm, staying calm, thankfully there was nothing left in my stomach to return, I looked from one to the other, "I'm not going to grow up to be a full-time math genius, whatever that looks like; I want a broader more varied experience. My first new subject addition will be for Josh to teach me to code this summer. He's had some success at a basic level, but I haven't grasped the more complex concepts, so that will be a challenge. Are we done?"

As I headed to my room, I heard my dad say, "That went better than expected." I paused, and I heard Mom say, "We're not done with the subject, and this fundraiser sounds like an excuse to hang out at that pool hall."

Dad said, "Dee, it's a restaurant."

Mom argued, "A restaurant with pool tables is a pool hall."

I was so upset that I went and called Cam to tell her about it. People are beginning to think my parents aren't so nice.

A Bad Joke Goes Bad

I was thrilled to be driving to school Thursday morning. I had some ridiculous fear my mother would say I couldn't go. Maybe I dreamed that during the night. I wanted to hug the building when I got there. I knew people when I was homeschooled, and I did things with groups of other kids, but I didn't have any friends. There were kids who were friends, so I'm not saying it was that way for everyone; it was just that way for me. Remember how I had only talked to Josh and no one else until I connected with Cam. So yeah, it was me. I don't want to go back to being that person.

When I got to the lunch table, I asked, "Does anybody know what the Spectrum Club is?"

Gene said, "We figured you would know."

I shook my head, "Not a clue?" Henry was a junior, so he didn't share our lunch time. He also left early most days because he got two class credits for working at the coffee shop. He had to write papers about management stuff.

Ashtyn said, "We are going to start visiting businesses this afternoon. Henry set up Eight Ball Sponsor for five hundred, Cue Ball Sponsors for two fifty, and Stripes or Solids for a hundred. There was a form you could print out to give to people."

Sean added, "I'm reaching out to the other high schools, public and private, to see if they want to put up a 'champion.' I figure, if we can book a 'champion' for each hour, we can draw in people from those schools. Coach Mayes gave me some names to contact. I figure, if we can get sports stars or other popular kids, it will be a better draw." About Coach, we are a STEAM school, so we don't have any teams, but we still have PE.

Rick suggested, "Go for the kids with the most Twitter followers."

Sean said, "I like it."

Shannon told us, "My dad belongs to a civic breakfast club, they have like fifty members. I'm going there before school on Tuesday to tell them about it. Dad says the club will probably give us five hundred, and we may pick up some sponsors. Everyone I'm introduced to, I'll ask individually, and then I get to talk to the club. The video on the website about how to do a pitch is excellent." Josh leaned over and whispered something to her that made her smile and her lights go bright.

I looked around the table, "I have to say I love each of you." I smiled and said, "Some more than others." I reached over and grabbed Josh's hand. Everyone but Cam thought that was hilarious. "Last night my parents suggested I should return to homeschooling."

Josh asked, "What did you do?"

"I regurgitated my whole dinner onto my plate, covered it with my napkin, and left the table."

Josh exclaimed, "You what?"

I repeated, "I threw up my dinner onto my plate."

Josh was all defensive, "I'm not a moron I know what regurgitate means; I just couldn't believe what you said."

Josh was beside me, I whispered to him, "I didn't mean anything. I know you're smart." He gave me a friendly punch.

Cam had come to sit beside me at this point, she said, "Tell them what you told your parents."

"After thirty minutes, I went out and told them I wasn't going back to homeschooling. I gave them some reasons, but you all are the real reason. I love having friends."

Josh was sitting on the opposite side of me from Cam, he nudged me with his elbow, "I think it's because you killed your brother." He thought he was funny. Most of the table said, "What?"

Cam lit into Josh, "You know that isn't true. You know the whole story isn't true. Why would you say something like that?"

Before Josh could return a defense, which probably would have been an attack, I very calmly said, "Stop. Josh, it was a dumb remark. Cam that's all it was. I love you, bro."

Gene raised his hand, not high in the air, like teacher look at me. He just held it up. "What's Josh talking about?"

I told them, "Someone is trolling me, sending texts and emails that say, 'Blotch is the mark of Cain.' They're coming from computers in the school library. They don't mean anything. I never had a brother. I didn't kill anyone."

Rick's friend Jesse said, "I work in the library, I can copy the computer user logs, and maybe we can figure out who it is."

I said, "Thanks, Jesse, I would appreciate it, but this isn't anything we're putting a lot of energy into."

When lunch was over, we stood up, and I made Cam hug Josh.

The Vision Leader

Friday night Josh stayed over because we were going to build the frame for his bed. Right now his mattress and box springs are sitting on the floor of my room. We started with breakfast. I had not made omelets since the morning in the fall when I asked about Blotch. This morning I loaded mine with onions, green peppers, bacon, and cheese. I topped it with salsa. I made everyone's the way they wanted it. Josh made the toast and poured juice. Mom made the coffee. It was a nice quiet breakfast. Afterward, we cleaned up before heading outside.

We pulled the cars out of the garage. Dad and I had previously cut the wood, so today Josh and I would sand and stain the wood. Dad came out to get us started. We each had a small electric sander. Dad told us, "The coarser the sandpaper, the lower the number; the finer the sandpaper, the higher number. Sand each side of each board with a 100 first, then 180 and finally a 220. When you're done with the sanding, come get me, and we'll move to the staining. Don't start staining without coming to get me."

Josh asked, "Why are these boards so thick?"

Dad explained, "When you buy one-inch lumber at the store, the board is really closer to three-quarters of an inch thick. I bought this as rough lumber and had them milled to a true inch. I think it makes the furniture look more massive. Perry's bed is built the same way."

Dad left, and we went to sanding, which is both boring and soothing. It took us a while to work through all the pieces. When we were done, I went and got Dad.

Dad said, "Now we have to get the garage as clean as we can. Josh, you can start by taking rags and wiping all the dust off the pieces of wood, while Perry starts sweeping and vacuuming."

When we thought we were done, Dad had us vacuum the pieces of wood and wipe them off again.

For staining, we put down drop cloths and put on plastic gloves. We were applying a mahogany stain to the oak wood to give it a dark color. You apply the stain, let it sit and then wipe off the excess stain. We had finished by lunch. After lunch, we would go add a second coat of stain. Dad said it makes for a deeper look to the wood.

When the second coat of staining was done, we headed to B and B to play pool. The doors had posters promoting the Big Hustle, 'The Blotch takes on all comers,' the date and time and how to make reservations. I said to Josh, "It seems like we ought to be doing something to work on the fundraiser."

Josh said, "We are. You're sharpening up your pool playing."

It was late afternoon, and there were a number of free tables, I said. "I was thinking of something more productive."

Josh went over to the rack to pick out a cue, "I assure you, somewhere someone is working on the fundraiser."

I racked up the balls, and we lagged to see who would go first. Josh won. I asked, "How can there be people working on the fundraiser who we don't even know, doing jobs we didn't even create?"

Josh took the break and sank a solid, he said, "When Demetri and I were meeting with Henry and Juan, the other webmaster, Henry said you were a Vision Leader."

Josh had missed, and I was shooting, but being a Vision Leader caused me to miss, "What?"

"Henry said that first night he caught the vision and went home and did the website, and it's been going like that ever since."

I asked, "What is the Spectrum Club?"

He shot and sank one, "They are kids at school with a family member, a relative, or a friend on the spectrum. They've each pledged to raise at least twelve hundred dollars in business sponsors. There are already a dozen club members."

I said, "I got distracted. Go back to being a Vision Leader."

Josh sank another ball, "You do realize I'm winning? Anyway, Henry said, you float a vision, and for many different reasons, people want to be a part of it. Look at the mean girls. Henry said the challenge is to keep things focused on your mission without doing anything to limit the potential of each joiner. I don't know what all is going on; I only know a lot is going on." After he paused for a while, he said, "So you don't get a swollen head, I think Henry is full of B.S., and it's all about Blotch. Somehow Blotch makes them feel guilty, and so out of guilt, they help."

I said, "You don't really believe that do you?"

He said, "No, I think Henry nailed it, I just don't want you getting a big head." Josh pointed toward the door with his pool cue, "Look who walked in."

Serena and Karalyne were heading toward us.

Karalyne pulled an outfit out of a bag, "Look at what we've got, silent auction stuff."

I said, "That's nice."

Serena added, "We go into the store, put together an outfit, ask for the manager, and ask them to donate it to the auction. They always say yes, at least so far, and then we have a form we give them. I always have someone in particular in mind or several people so that I can encourage them to bid. We are also going to have a buy for this price option that is like ten percent more than the item is worth."

Josh said, "This is so great. Thank you, girls."

Karalyne said, "Our whole table is out working it tonight. It's like shopping for free."

Karalyne was standing a little too close to me and making me very nervous. "This is so good of you girls."

Standing shoulder to shoulder with me and holding up a different outfit she asked, "Perry, don't you think I would be cute in this."

She really was way too close. I stammered, "I think you would look great in that."

Karalyne blushed, "Oh Perry, I don't mean to make you nervous. I know you're with Cam," she passed her fingertips across Blotch, "I would never want to come between you and her."

Serena said, "Come on Karalyne, we have a few more stores to hit bye boys."

Karalyne said, "We're heading to Duluth Trading to see if we can find something Cam would bid on."

Josh turned to me, "Whew, those girls are mean and hot."

Out of nowhere Cam and Shannon were there. Shannon asked, "What girls are hot?"

Cam asked, "What girls are mean?"

What do you say? Is there a way out of this? I have a feeling we're not going to finish this game of pool, then I saw, they're faces were straight and serious, but their lights were laughing. "You set us up didn't you? You sent them in here to mess with us."

Now they were cracking up. Cam said, "You two looked like kids caught with their hands in the cookie jar."

Josh hugged Shannon. I heard him say, "They aren't as hot as you, but they sure are mean."

I managed to lean in and give Cam a small kiss. We went and got a table to start a night out with our girls.

Sean's Big News

We assembled Josh's bed on Sunday and moved it into our bedroom. He went home Sunday afternoon after we worked on his Algebra. Monday lunch was great because people had been saving news to share.

Cam started, "McDerman Pool Cues has signed on as the lead sponsor at a thousand dollars. All they want is for us to add their logo to the posters, website, and any other publicity. Also, they want us to add a tagline to the title, 'Blotch and the McDerman C21 vs. All Comers.'"

I asked, "How did that happen?"

Cam answered, "The manager at the sporting goods store took care of all of it. They also gave us four pool cues to use in the auction or as prizes."

I said, "I can tell that's not the whole story."

Cam replied, "I know you can tell that's not the whole story, but that's all the story I'm going to tell. So Josh if you would take care of the website, I already told the other PR people."

I asked, "What other PR people?"

Josh said, "The PR team is divided into website, social media, print, and press releases."

I asked, "Who is doing all that?"

Sean said, "The vision team continues to expand."

Gene added, "We got five sponsors last Friday, Ashtyn is a natural salesperson. We would have gotten more, but we got distracted." He nuzzled into Ashtyn's neck.

Rick asked, "Did you turn those into the treasurer?"

Ashtyn replied, "Two went online to give, but we turned in the checks from the others and all the paperwork."

Rick said, "I know they have a goal of having all the sponsors up to date on the website by Friday."

I asked, "We have a treasurer?"

Rick said, "The treasurer from the Renaissance Center board is serving as treasurer for the fundraiser."

Sean jumped in, "Well I have some news. I managed to track down somebody at each of the three nearest high schools, and they gave me leads to the people with the most online followers, so I checked them out online and picked the ones I thought looked like the biggest draw. I have three different high schools with buy-in, and as that word spreads today, you should see a push in table reservations."

Cam said, "Sean, that is great! Now tell him the catch. Tell him."

Sean smiled, "Two of them are girls, and the deal is if they beat you, they get to kiss you."

I turned bright red.

Cam said, "As far as I am concerned, they can do anything they want to try to distract you. Maybe we ought to offer Karalyne the same deal."

Everyone hooted and hollered at that. Josh said, "She'd make a big donation for that opportunity." Everyone hooted and hollered some more. (Hooted and Hollered?)

I said to Cam, "Are you just going to throw me to the wolves?"

Cam nodded, "Maybe you're just more man than I can manage. Plus you're so handsome when you blush. Also, I know they can't distract you."

I turned bright red.

Sean said, "Now for my big announcement. Drum roll, please."

Rick said, "No, tell them the other big announcement."

Now Sean blushed as everyone was saying, "Come on share."

He said, "Okay, okay, I got a date. Since I know the first thing you all want to ask is does she know, the answer is yes. She was online checking me out as we talked. You don't have to be a master detective to figure it out, and I purposely didn't do anything to hide it." Have I told you Sean used to be Sarai, but like Ashtyn he came back after Christmas break as Sean?

Shannon said, "Sean that is great! Now, what can be bigger news than that."

He said, "Drum roll, please." All the guys did finger drums on the table. "I had a call Saturday afternoon from Congressmen Ailey's office. He wants to come play you. It will be a huge draw. They said as we get closer, they can give us an idea of when he can be there, but they assured me he would come, and we can use his name in publicity."

Shannon asked, "Anyone know how that happened?"

Ashtyn in a tiny voice said, "I do." Everyone turned to her. "Slider asked him. It seems that motorcycles are one of the great equalizers. You know, something that brings people together across various boundaries.

Anyway, they ride together, so Slider asked him, and he said he would be glad to."

Sean added, "The staff guy said the Congressman would want to congratulate Mrs. Patel for the Block Grant she got. Apparently, he had something to do with that."

Cam was looking at me and reading my face, "What?"

I said, "I'll tell you later." She has gotten way too good at reading my facial expressions. I told the group "I plan to go to the center this afternoon. Mrs. Patel will be excited to hear how well we're doing."

Josh said, "I don't think that is such a good idea."

I looked at him, "Why?"

Cam jumped in, "I thought this afternoon, we should look at what you'll wear."

I said, "We have plenty of time for that; I don't need to wear anything special."

Cam said, "Everything needs attention. What if you need to order some clothes?"

Shannon agreed, "Yeah, Cam and I will come to your house this afternoon and check out your closet."

I said, "I was just going to swing by on my way to meet my mother for an appointment with her counselor. So if there's a reason you don't want me to go to the center, I won't go."

Josh said, "That sounds good. You can go tomorrow."

I found out later that they were filming the videos of Pah and Marlin that afternoon.

Mom is Dating an Eighteen Year Old

As I was walking into the counseling center, my phone beeped with a message, 'Blotch = Mark of Cain.' Somehow this guy knows how to poke me when I have the most going on. Mom was sitting in the waiting area. We sat there for an uncomfortable ten minutes before the counselor called us into her office. She was maybe fifty. She said, "Call me Dissanna." Is that the same as saying my name is Dissanna, or is she saying I like to be called Dissanna?

There was some make-Perry-comfortable talk, "there's nothing to be afraid of," and "honesty helps heal." I didn't like her lights. She wasn't genuinely talking to me; she was drawing comparisons between what my mother had said about me and what she was seeing. We talked through some of the things that had happened in the past six months. We talked about how much change there had been in our family and in my life and the stress of my various hospitalizations. In our conversation, we made it to the day Mom said I couldn't have Blotch removed which lead to the night I didn't come home. I told them I wouldn't apologize for not coming home and I was sorry that Mom felt hurt when I turned off my phone, but I wouldn't apologize for that either. I thought she should apologize for banishing me from home for a week afterward. I didn't tell them that either. I spent the week with Josh.

I think we were three-quarters of the way through our hour when Dissanna said, "Perry is there anything you want to say to your mother?"

I found the courage to ask, "Mom, why are you mad at me?" I expected her to say, 'Love, I'm not mad at you.'

Instead, she looked at Dissanna who said, "You should tell him, just like we have talked about."

This is what I heard.

Mom turned to me, "Perry, I am mad, but it's not at you and any part that I project that way is wrong. When you were homeschooling and excelling in everything, you seemed so set apart, and above all the other kids I saw. I felt that what I had given up was worth it. Now you seem ordinary, and you don't want to spend your life being a math genius. I'm feeling cheated."

I was confused, "What are you talking about?"

She said, "Perry, I gave up my young adulthood. When other kids were going for a beer on Friday afternoon, I was heading home to change diapers. It all seemed so worth it until this year. I know you didn't ask me to give up anything. I know I chose. Now I wonder if I chose wrong. And, in another very short three years, you'll be heading off to college and where will I be?"

I was in shock. Dissanna sat there smiling; my mother looked sad. They acted like it was my turn to open up. I had some thoughts, but none would contribute to any healing. I sat in silence. Let me list for you; I didn't ask to be born. I didn't ask to be homeschooled. I didn't ask to not go to daycare or after-school care. I didn't ask for any of this.

I spoke, "I appreciate all you have done for me, Mom. I am sorry if you are disappointed in me, but

Mom I can't do anything about the last sixteen years, but I can do all in my power to enable you to do whatever you're ready to do going forward, just like I know you and Dad will support me in my future choices. I'm here for you as long as it's not leaving Dad or me. I will fight for our family. I am fighting for our family."

Dissanna and Mom sat there looking at me.

Dissanna said, "Our hour is up. Dee and I will have to take this up next week."

As far as I was concerned, we were being dumped out on the street in the middle of something, but Mom seemed happy with where things were, Dissanna said, "Perry thank you for coming today. We made some real progress."

I felt I had been told I had ruined my mother's life and my future appeared to her as a mediocre disappointment. I was certain sharing that was not going to help, but that's what I felt.

In the waiting area, we ran into Tristan. Remember Tristan, he's a senior in my math class or maybe better said I'm a freshman in his senior math class. After he almost killed me when I let him pound my stomach, my mother decided she liked him. (It's a long story.) He lit up with positive light when he saw my mother. Mom said, "Oh Tristan how was your session today?"

He said, "Excellent, Dee. Perry, what did you think of Dissanna? I've seen her when my counselor, Jarrod, was out of town. I think she is very insightful."

A shiver ran through me. I hoped it didn't show, "She definitely surprised me with some of her insights."

Tristan said, "Great! Dee, I have to run, but maybe next week, we can go for coffee."

Mom, my Mom, right in front of me said, "I'd like that, Tristan." And he was gone.

I turned and looked at Mom, "You just made a date to go get coffee with Tristan."

Mom said, "Yes, but not a date. We've done it before. We share insights into what we are working on."

I was astounded, "Have you shared with Tristan what you are feeling about me?"

She said, "No, I wouldn't do that."

I was so on the edge of losing it, "Does Dad know you and Tristan are dating?"

Mom had this look that went with what she was about to say, "Perry, you are so silly. I am not dating Tristan, and yes, your dad knows I have had coffee with Tristan."

It was taking all my mental strength to hold myself together. I had so much going on in my head and a clueless mother, who didn't realize she had just dealt her son a devastating blow in the counseling session and that there was an eighteen-year-old who had more on his mind than coffee. "Mom, you know how Dad, in his way, is trying to teach me some things about relationships and women?"

"Yes."

I was so calm, "So eighteen-year-old boys have only one motivation for talking to women, only one. They may not act on that one motivation, but it doesn't mean it isn't their one motivation."

Mom looked at me like I was ridiculous, "Perry, that is not true, and it's not true of Tristan."

I said, "I'm going to leave before my head explodes, but Mom think about what I've said. Ask Dad about it. Meeting with Tristan is not a good thing." I left. I was glad I had my own wheels.

The Man is Still Angry

I needed to go clear my head. In books, the guys all have a secluded place no one else knows about where they go look out over the ocean or the lake, and all comes clear. Often a beautiful girl shows up. My head cleared enough to point me toward Green Lake Park. I parked and headed down toward the lake. I sat on the picnic table where Cam and I had studied.

Let me review for you:
  1.   I am a disappointment to my mother.
  2.   My mother feels I ruined her life.
  3.   My mother is dating a high school senior and won't admit it.

I want to go back in the hospital. Let's review the positives of going into the hospital:
  1. I get at least twenty-four hours sleep.
  2. All decisions are made for me.
  3. Everyone feels sorry for me.
  4. Everyone rallies around.
  5. When I get out, all the problems are solved.
The problem is I'm not sick.

I was awakened from my stupor by Sadie licking my hands. Except, we know it's not Sadie. I looked up to see Frisbee man who's not. Marlin's dad. "(The sign for Perry) rough day, huh kid."

"You're not Marlin's dad."

"I never said I was."

I petted the dog, "Is this Sadie?"

"Yes."

I asked, "How is that?"

He said, "It just is."

"Who are you?"

He said, "I just am."

I told him, "You are as informative as a school resource officer. Why are you here?"

He was all serious now, his look and his tone bordered on angry, "Here is how it is. You can't fix everything, but you still have time to save the fundraiser. The fundraiser is the answer to everything."

I told him, "The fundraiser is running itself. I'm the Vision Leader."

He was way too intense, "If you don't act in the next few hours, it's going to collapse. Start by thanking people. Everything hinges on the fundraiser."

I was annoyed by this guy who knew way too much about me and wouldn't even tell me his name, "Are we talking apocalyptic end of the world? Earthquakes releasing dragons that devour all humanity?"

He wasn't laughing, "You're a real funny kid. I'm talking you, your family, the Renaissance Center. Yes, you are the Vision Leader, but it doesn't mean you don't have work to do. You need to be thanking people and paying attention to details."

I looked at the ground, shaking my head, "Man you are trying to put…" I looked up, but he and Sadie were gone.

Here is the learning, justt because someone annoys you or even pisses you off, it doesn't necessarily mean they were wrong. Maybe it was my job to pay attention to details and to thank people. I headed home to do just that.

Mom had picked up Chinese food, and Dad was going to be late, so she said I could make a plate and eat in my room. I was glad the guy in the park had wiped away any focus on the counseling session. I knew I would have to think through that stuff, but I was thankful to not be doing it right then. I brought the volunteer page of the website up on my computer.

Starting with Henry, I texted everyone, including Josh and Cam. I thanked people, even when I didn't know what they were doing. Like there was a band coordinator? I didn't have a clue. There were close to fifty volunteers listed. I wasn't even halfway through when texts started coming back. People were reporting their accomplishments vs. their goals. Five people in the Spectrum Club had met their goals and doubled them. Sarena, Karalyne and the mean girls had seventy-five percent participation from mall stores and were working on the other twenty-five percent. The people signing up sponsors reported how many sponsors they had signed and in what categories. The video team had made three promotional videos, but they didn't say of what. I had started at six-thirty, and I finished at nine. I lay down on my bed exhausted.

The word details flashed into my head. I went back to my computer. I set up several spreadsheets to track all the data I had received. The first spreadsheet was a listing of all the volunteers, their job, a check that they had been contacted, and another column to track if they got back to me. I was at this point, at a forty-five percent response. I then set up a spreadsheet for the sixteen people recruiting sponsors, tracking which category the sponsor had pledged. Josh sent me a read out from the reservation app reporting how many parties had made reservations, how many in each party and for which time slots. Reservations were twenty dollars per party whether there is one or six in the party. The band coordinator reported she had three bands from our school and was working on three other bands. One group per hour for the six hours of the fundraiser was her goal. They would play in the mall outside the restaurant where the silent auction would be set up because apparently there was not enough room in the restaurant for the silent auction.

At ten thirty I went to shower. In the shower, it dawned on me. I needed to respond to the people who had texted back. After my shower, I set my alarm for six a.m., put my phone on silent, and texted goodnight to Cam and Josh.

Six a.m. I looked at my phone; forty of the forty-eight people I texted the night before had texted back. I started replying to their texts with specific praise for their accomplishments and charting the ones I had not charted previously.

By the time I needed to dress for school, I was only halfway through. As I got to school, I got a text from Henry, 'Last night some people were in the shop complaining that they were volunteering in the Big Hustle, but you ignored them in the hall. I explained that you knew all their names but didn't know faces. Be more friendly.' This had been what was unraveling. I hadn't even made it to the school building, and a girl said, "Hi Perry, I'm Rebecca," and I was able to say, "Video Team or Spectrum Club Rebecca." She replied, "Spectrum club." I said, "Thanks, you're already at your goal, and you doubled it. That's powerful."

And it went on like that. I think before lunch I had talked to over half the volunteers. The most embarrassing was when I was at the urinal peeing. It is an unwritten rule that you don't talk to the guy at the next urinal while you're peeing. The rule gets broken a lot, but it is a rule. The guy next to me said, "Hey Blotch thanks for what you're doing."

I looked over at him, It's also very important you keep your eyes up, "Are you helping? I know names but not faces."

He said, "Yeah, I'm Nicholas."

I was able to say, "You started the Spectrum Club, thanks. The team is doing great work."

He volunteered, "My cousin is on the spectrum. He's smart, but loud noises send him over the top. Anyway thanks."

We both finished and left.

You, Come With Me

As I am sure you have noticed, I haven't told anyone about the counseling session nor about the man, not Marlin's dad, in the park. I don't want to tell them. Cam still shows up late most of the time, so I spent the first ten minutes of lunch responding to messages, praising and thanking people. I had also used the time between classes, and I was at least current for the moment.

Cam arrived, she set her books down across the table from me. "Someone lit a fire under you. Did you text the whole school last night?"

I laughed, "Only all the volunteers. You all know I appreciate everything you're doing, but I hadn't told everyone else. There is an amazing amount of stuff going on. Did you know we have bands?"

Everyone said, "Yes."

I asked, "Okay, did you know the Shadowman Band is playing the last hour and their drummer, Terry, is on the spectrum?"

Josh said, "Okay that is news, and that will pack the place. People love the ShadowMan Band. Did you know they started in coffee shop Henry's garage?" People didn't know that.

Everyone talked about what they were doing, what other exciting news they had, and we talked about regular school stuff. I had finished eating. Cam only had yogurt, so she was done. Lunch wasn't half over, and she gathered up our trash and took it to the can. She had never done that before. She came back to the table, pointed at me, and said, "You, come with me." She picked up her book bag, so I picked up mine and followed her out of the cafeteria. Everyone at the table was as stunned as I was.

We went and sat on a bench in the courtyard away from everyone else. She was facing me, "So what is it?"

She can read me so well there was no way to deny it, "I went to Green Lake yesterday afternoon, and the Frisbee guy showed up. He said the dog was Sadie, but that he never claimed he was Marlin's dad. I asked how could this be Sadie, and he said she just was. He wouldn't tell me his name. He was angry. He said everything depended on the fundraiser, I needed to pay attention to details, and I needed to thank people. And then he was gone."

She asked, "What do you mean gone?"

I told her, "I looked down at the ground, halfway through telling him he was putting a lot on my shoulders, I looked up, and he was gone. I was pissed and angry, but I decided he was right, so I went home and started my thank you blitz."

She shook her head, "Who is this guy who runs around with a ghost dog?"

I said, "I wish I knew."

She continued, "So speaking of details why did you have that look at lunch yesterday when Sean mentioned the Block Grant?"

I told her, "Mrs. Patel told me part of their financial troubles were that they didn't get the Block Grant."

She said, "Maybe there were two different grants, and she got one but not the other."

I said, "You're right. I'll ask her."

She changed her position, "So you haven't said anything to Josh or me about the counseling session."

I said, "It was bad."

She asked, "How bad?"

I told her, "If I start talking, I'll just start crying."

She moved close enough to put a hand on my shoulder, "Is it so bad you can't tell Josh or me?"

"Yes."

She said, "You need to talk to someone."

"Who?"

She said, "Your Doctor said you could talk to him anytime."

"I don't have an appointment."

She let out a sigh, "You call his office and make one." She took my phone, typed in his name, dialed the number and handed it back to me."

"Hi, I'm Perry Larcon, I'm a patient, I need an appointment to talk with Dr. Pender, he said I could call, fifteen to twenty minutes, it's a nine."

Cam yelled toward the phone, "It's a full-on ten plus."

I said, "Okay," and hung up. "They are going to talk to him and get back to me."

She asked, "See it's not just hanging there anymore, you have a plan to address it. You feel better don't you?"

Not one to miss an opportunity, I leaned in for a kiss. When we pulled apart, she asked, "Was this all a set up so you could get a kiss?"

I laughed, "I wish that were true."

They called while I was in class and left a message. He was going to see his mother in the afternoon; remember she lives on my street. I could meet him in her driveway at four-thirty. Between classes, I called to say that would work.

Dr. Pender had just arrived as I pulled up behind him. We went and sat on the porch steps. He said, "If you are here to hit me up for the fundraiser, I already pledged as a cue ball sponsor."

I laughed, "Thanks, I wish that was it. So to cut to the chase, yesterday I went to a session with my mother and her counselor. My mother said things that hurt so much I couldn't even bring myself to share them with my friends."

I could tell he was really listening to me, "Have you talked to your mother about what she said since then?"

I shook my head, "No, I couldn't bring myself to do that either."

He asked, "Do you want to tell me what she said?"

"No, I really don't."

He accepted that, "At my office, I have a handout for almost everything that a patient comes in for, do you know why?"

I laughed, "You own stock in a printing company."

He smiled, "No, because I can't control what people hear. This often happens with severe illnesses. The doctor gives a good explanation of what is happening, but the patient only hears part of it. The patient hears, 'your leg is going to be as good as new', but what the doctor said was 'If you lose twenty pounds and follow this six-month course of physical therapy, your leg should be as good as new.'"

I said, "I get it, but what do I do?"

He told me, "You get together with your mother and tell her about this conversation, then tell her what you heard, then let her respond. If what she says makes you feel better tell her. If it doesn't, tell her that also. Do you think you can do that?"

I said, "I can do it."

He replied, "See you at the Big Hustle."

Does My Mother Love Me?

Mom and I already planned to make pork chops together on Wednesday, so I put off our talk until then. The only thing was Cam was coming for dinner, and then we were going to study. So maybe it would depend on whether talking made things better or not. We dip the pork chops in milk and eggs, coat them with a mixture of baking mix, bread crumbs, and seasoning, and then we put them in a skillet to brown them on both sides. When they are ready, we put them in a baking dish and put them in the oven for an hour. If you leave them uncovered, they are crispy; if you cover them they; aren't. We cover ours.

When we had them in the oven, I found the courage to say, "Mom, can we talk about the counseling session?"

She sat down at the table, "Sure sweetie, I thought it went well, didn't you?"

I sat across from her, "Mom, I was devastated by what you said. I couldn't even tell Cam or Josh about it."

She reached over and grabbed my hand, "Why sweetie?"

I took a deep breath, "So yesterday I spoke to Dr. Pender," that surprised her. "He said I should tell you what I heard, which might be quite different than what you said. He says this happens all the time."

Mom said, "Yes, that's true, so what did you hear?"

I said, "This is going to be very hard, so please let me finish," She nodded to say okay. "I heard you say, you gave up so much to have me, and you are sorry for that choice. When you thought I was extra special, you felt it might be worth it, but now you think I'm making mediocre choices about my life, and you feel like you wasted the last sixteen years of your life." I had started with angry energy, but as I listened to what I was saying I began to work hard not to cry. What I had heard was that my mother didn't love me. If I said that out loud, I felt I would just dissolve into a pile of tears.

Mom sat there looking at me. A tear rolled down her cheek.

"Mom, talk to me."

She grabbed both my hands, "It breaks my heart that you heard that, that you have been carrying that around for two days. Perry, I love you more than my own life. I have never regretted for one moment my decision to marry your father nor our decision to have you. I cherish every day I've been with you, and those experiences mean more to me than any college or young adult thing I missed out on. I see Dissanna for a number of reasons, but one is, this has been a difficult year for me. For the first time, you have a life totally apart and separate from me. Maybe for most families, it happens gradually, but for us, it seems like last September, you started public school, and then you were gone. In some very dysfunctional way, the three times you ended up in the hospital, and I almost lost you, also meant that you were my little boy who needed me."

What she said felt good, but I had questions, "What about the anger?"

She looked down, "Sometimes I'm angry, yes. Sometimes you get it, and sometimes I lash out at your dad. My anger comes from my fear of what will happen as you move further away from me, as you head off to college and my fear of what happens to your dad and me as you move off into your own life. None of that is to say you shouldn't be moving up and off into your own life."

I was on the edge of crying. I don't think most boys have talks like these with their mothers. "Mom, I am moving off into my own life, but I will always be your son. I will always love you. I will always need you." We sat in silence for a few moments, I found the courage to ask one last question, "Mom if you love me so much why did I have to stay at Josh's that week?"

She was sad, "That was a horrible week. I can't imagine what Josh's parents and any of your friends' parents think of us."

I told her, "You may not know, but Cam wouldn't talk to me that week either."

She said, "I'm so sorry. That Saturday morning when I told your dad not to bring you home, I was angry, and I was hurt. I felt, 'Perry's going to leave one day; why doesn't he just be gone now.' It was a terrible feeling. Your dad agreed to it because he knew we all needed a cooling off period, so we would quit hurting each other. My heart hurt that whole week."

We had reached a good place, "Mom, is it still okay if Cam comes for supper and to study? I could go meet her at the library after supper if you would rather."

Mom said, "It is still good, but I have two more things I want to share. Your dad and I talked and think you are a little right about the Tristan thing. Tristan has done nothing inappropriate, nor do I think he might, but there is the potential for misunderstanding, so I'm moving my appointment to another time, and that will solve the problem." I nodded yes. "Also in a few weeks, your dad and I would like to go away on a couples' retreat. Would that be okay?"

I said, "Sure, I'll stay at the Benton's; it'll be fine."

She said, "The thing is we have to turn in our phones when we arrive on Friday, and we don't get them back until Sunday afternoon."

I didn't like that at all, but I told her, "Mom, I'm sixteen; I'll be fine."

"Good, I'll go freshen up if you will finish up dinner and set the table."

Did I Kill My Brother?

The four of us sat down for supper at six thirty. Cam and I talked a lot about the Big Hustle. Mom and Dad were both impressed by what we were accomplishing. As we were finishing eating, Cam said, "Ms. Larcon, there is something Perry would like to ask you."

Mom and Dad both looked at me. I glared at Cam. "Cam, this is not the time." I was trying not to betray how angry I was. This was stepping over the line.

Mom said, "Perry, I've learned in counseling about safe places, and this is a safe place for you to ask us anything. Having worked through Blotch and so many other things has proven we can talk about anything that concerns any of us."

This psychobabble was not helping. My chest was tightening. How do I open? I was not prepared for this. "Someone is trolling me."

Dad asked, "What does that mean?"

I said, "They're sending me harassing emails and texts. All they say is 'Blotch equals the mark of Cain.'"

Mom and Dad looked at each other. Cam and I both saw it. Dad looked down at his plate, and asked, "What do you think that means?"

I was becoming thankful Cam forced this, there was apparently something here. I asked, "Did I kill my brother?"

Mom in a scarily calm way said, "Perry, the doctors were quite clear you had nothing to do with your brother's death. Now if you'll excuse me, I'm going to

my room. Your father can answer any other questions."
Mom got up and left.

Cam, Dad and I looked at each other. Cam and I sat
in stunned silence.

"Dad?"

Dad took a deep breath, "You had a twin brother.
His heart stopped beating three months into the
pregnancy. It was sad. No one outside the family or the
doctor's office would know about this."

I was stunned, "Was it my fault?"

Dad reached out and grabbed my hand, "No Perry.
Like your mother said, the doctors were very clear it
wasn't your fault."

I asked, "Why did you never tell me?"

"Perry, how would that have been good? I think we
made the wrong choice to not talk about Blotch, but here
I think we made the right choice."

I thought maybe he was right. "Is there anything else
I don't know?"

Dad laughed, "Probably, but I don't know what it is.
I'm going to go see about your mother. In the future
could you run things by me before you spring them on
us?"

Cam and I cleared the table and loaded the
dishwasher. We went upstairs to my room. I laid down
on my bed, "Will you come lay beside me?"

She walked toward me, "That's against the rules."
She lay beside me resting her head on my chest. I played
with her hair.

I said, "We'll hear them if they come upstairs."

She asked, "What are you feeling?"

I said, "I'm stunned. I'm shocked. Maybe that emptiness I feel sometimes is where my brother should be."

She can be so wonderful, "I think Josh is your missing twin, your real brother." I was silent. "Do you know any other guys in ninth grade who regularly have sleepovers? Do you know any other guys who demand their parents put an extra bed in their bedroom for their best friend?"

I said, "No."

She rose up to look me in the eye, "Unless you're crawling into bed with him at night."

I calmly told her, "Josh and I are not crawling into bed together."

She stroked my hair, "I'm jealous; he has a bed here, and I don't."

I told her, "Half of this one is yours." And we kissed.

No studying was done.

I'm Behind in School

Thursday afternoon and evening I focused on school. I was a little behind on various assignments, so I made up a study schedule using twenty-minute study units. During the five minute breaks, I let myself answer messages. I had severely increased my workload by messaging everyone, but it had also increased productivity. We had also added ten volunteers since I had started being more engaged. On one of my breaks, I texted Cam.

'I'm on a study break.'

'We should have an appreciation mixer mingle for all the volunteers. Ideas?'

I went back to work. At my next break I found:

'Coffee shop, Monday evening 7 - 8.'

I texted, 'Did you ask Henry?'

'Duh, Of course, I did.'

'You, Josh, Shannon and I will bake brownies at my house Sunday afternoon.'

I texted, 'You're amazing.'

I went to sleep knowing I had gotten a handle on the thank you side of my assignment, but I wasn't sure I had a grip on my details assignment. When I woke up, I knew I needed to talk to Henry and Ms. Patel. I texted both. By the time I got to school, I had a meeting with Henry right after school and then Ms. Patel after that.

Henry told me to get to the coffee shop as soon after school as possible because Friday afternoons get busy early. I managed to get out of my last class ten minutes early. We sat down at a table. Henry asked, "Have you thought about a job?"

I laughed because I had so much else on my mind, "In the middle of everything else, I actually have. I think I am going to apply at one of the smaller hardware stores. Not one of the box stores but the small ones that help people solve their problems."

Henry only asked, "Why?"

I laughed again because I knew he would ask, and I was ready, "First I'll learn to work with customers, Second, I'll develop a broad understanding of the basic things people need to know about where they live. Third I'll learn about tools."

Henry said, "Very good, you don't need to stay there more than three to six months. Now, what did you need to see me about that couldn't wait?"

I blurted it out, "What do you know about embezzlement?"

He didn't even ask why. "I deal with stealing. Stealing is when someone with whom you have a nominal relationship takes something from you. Here it may be a customer shoplifting or an employee. Because of the value of our products, it's usually about twenty dollars a hit, though I had one employee try to take a whole case of coffee. Embezzlement is committed by someone in your inner circle of trust. They have to have access to the bank accounts and the flow of information. In a small organization, that usually means the person in charge, the treasurer or the bookkeeper. In a larger organization, it may all be within the accounting department. For embezzlement to be ongoing, they have to have a way to get the money out and a way to cover what is missing."

I asked, "How do you catch them?"

Henry said, "If there's smoke there's usually fire."

I asked, "What does that mean?"

He laughed, "It means don't ignore little things that seem wrong. Don't be put off by easy answers. Dig deeper and make sure nothing is wrong. It's better to look and find nothing than to not look."

I went over to the center to see Ms. Patel. We sat in her office. I told her all about what was going on with the fundraiser and how we were looking at income streams at this point moving into the high twenty thousand but it was still possible we could hit forty thousand, She was very appreciative, then I went looking for fire. "The Entrepreneur Center teacher said I could earn a certificate of recognition if I wrote up the fundraiser and added information about business operations, so I was wondering if you could answer some questions?"

"Sure Perry, what can I tell you?"

I had a pad for taking notes to make this look real, "How are you funded?"

I could tell money was a worrisome subject to her, "Most of our money comes from school funds; like a charter school, we are paid so much per student for the allotted number of school days. Parents pay a fee for summer and non-school days. Some money then comes from community organizations, our annual fundraiser, and then the block grant we didn't get." This was what I wanted to see. She was telling the truth. I was so glad to see that.

I asked, "Do you have a bookkeeper to track all that."

She smiled, "I am so lucky. Our board treasurer, Mr. Vinton, acts as our bookkeeper, our administrator, and all-around office person."

I had what I needed, a suspect. I headed home to get cleaned up. I had a date with Cam in the evening. Remember, 'clean boys aren't always lucky boys, but smelly boys are rarely lucky boys.'

He's a Mall Cop, He Had a Taser

Most people are going to think this is the lamest date, but it's what Cam wanted to do. We went to the food court at the mall for dinner. Cam loves the bourbon chicken the Chinese place has. Sometimes she will stand there like she is trying to make up her mind and keep asking for samples until they cut her off. This one guy recognizes her and won't give her any.

After our not gourmet meal, she wanted to go to the arcade to play skeeball. She loves skeeball more than bourbon chicken. The reason is she is better at skeeball than I am. So beating me, while racking up all her tickets and all my tickets, is for her a delightful evening. After an hour of playing skeeball, we went to cash in our tickets. She was looking at all the trinkets and stuffed animals, and I was trying to act interested, and suddenly she burst into tears and ran out into the mall. Before I turned to follow, my eyes landed on the problem, a stuffed dog that looked unbelievably like her dog Showey who had died last year.

I ran out into the mall. I couldn't see her anywhere. I started running through the mall. I circled back to the food court. I thought about the girl's bathroom. I went and stood outside it. When two girls came out, I asked them, "Is there another girl in there, maybe crying? I'm looking for my girlfriend?"

They looked at me and at Blotch, "Listen creep if she doesn't want to be found, you should beat it."

Wow, I didn't see that coming. I called her phone; it went right to voicemail. It was the kind of restroom without a door, so I called out, "Cam, I understand. Come talk to me." A couple of women walked past me into the restroom.

The mall cop showed up, "What are you doing here kid?"

I told him, "My girlfriend got upset, and she ran into the restroom."

He cracked his knuckles and then rested a hand on his taser, "What'd you do punk?"

I told him, "I didn't do anything. She saw a stuffed animal that looked like her dog that died, and she got upset."

"Oh, kid, I hope you write stories because you're good at it. I remember you; you're the kid who almost started that fight at Billiards a couple of months ago. Look, I'm not going to ban you from the mall, yet, but you need to go ahead and leave tonight."

I called out, "Cam, please come out. They're throwing me out of the mall. Please."

She walked out of the restrooms all smiles, like nothing had happened, "Oh officer thank you for finding him. I've been looking all over for him." She took my arm, and we headed for the exit. There was a poster of me at the front of Burgers and Billiards. I don't know why but I got butterflies in my stomach.

As soon as we stepped out of the mall, she burst out laughing. She pointed at me, "When I came out of the restroom, I thought I was going to find you in handcuffs. You sounded so pitiful, and you looked so scared standing there by that mall cop. Perry, he was a mall cop."

In my defense, I said, "He had a Taser." She was so happy, but I don't know what I felt, "So you staged all this so you could play me?"

She said, "Who do you think called mall security?"

We were in the Jeep, "The mean girls who called me creepy is who I thought called him."

She leaned over and touched my face, "Did some mean girls call you creepy?"

I said, "Yes," and leaned in for a kiss. She let me kiss her. We kissed long enough to fog up the windows. When we realized it, we both started laughing. My parents had twice fogged up their car windows waiting for me outside Cam's house.

We were still sitting in the parking lot, I was holding her hand, "Do you want to talk about Showey?"

Simply and abruptly she said, "No."

I asked, "Was it really you who called security?"

She said, "No, but I wish it had been."

It was open mike night at the coffee shop, so we went there.

Trouble Finds Perry

For the past few Saturdays, I had been going to Billiards before they opened to practice. There is a back door where the dumpsters are, and I enter there with the rest of the staff. They start arriving around nine thirty I go in at ten, and the restaurant opens at eleven.

This day I picked up Ashtyn on my way. Gene was going to meet her at the mall at noon. "How are you and Gene doing?"

She smiled. She had a beautiful smile, "We're great. He's so nice. Slider finally lets us go out by ourselves." They had been on supervised dating while everyone tried to decide if Gene could be trusted. "You know he never complained about any of that. How are you and Cam?"

I thought about last night and the mall cop, "Oh we are our usual selves. Last night we were here, and she called the mall cop on me, but other than that we're good. She got upset and ran into the girl's room; I was outside calling for her to come out. I really think it was these girls who called me creepy who called security. Like I said, it's never dull."

At the mall, the dumpster area was surrounded by a wall so you wouldn't see the dirty stuff. This is also where deliveries are made. We walked into the enclosure, and there was Skulls. Skulls and I had a run in at Billiards and Burgers one night. I beat him badly at the game. He was so mad he slammed a cue against the table splintering it. He was there with his wingman between us and the door. I turned to Ashtyn, "Run, they only want me, run." She hesitated and then took off. I was half the size of these two guys, and she was half my size. She needed to save herself.

Skulls said, "So you are quite the pool star. I've seen your little movie and posters for your little hustle."

He was walking toward me, the wingman working his way behind me. "I didn't hustle you, man, and I offered you your money back."

The wingman grabbed me from behind and threw my pool cue to Skulls. He had horrible breath. I decided mentioning that fact would not help my situation. Skulls started assembling my cue. I totally lost my commitment to non-violence. I hated him. I struggled to get free. Skulls said, "Maybe this is a magic pool cue and if it's gone so will be the super pool player." He whacked the pool cue against a dumpster, splintering the smaller half into multiple pieces. A shiver ran through me. I struggled in vain to get free. I wanted at him. Skulls gave the nod to his wingman who shoved me against one of the dumpsters. He pushed my right hand out into the air, but my arm was firmly pinned to the dumpster. Skulls had the remaining part of the cue as a club. They were going to shatter my hand. I closed my eyes as tight as I could. I heard Skulls scream and then the wingman. My eyes were burning. Someone grabbed my hand and pulled me away.

My eyes were stinging and watering. "What is happening?" I realized Ashtyn was leading me out into the parking lot. I couldn't open my eyes. The whole parking lot started roaring.

I couldn't keep my eyes open.

Ashtyn sat me down by a tree in the parking lot, "Stay here you're safe. Hold on to this tree; I'll be right back." I wrapped my arms around the tree. Tears were pouring out of my eyes. She ran off shouting over the noise, "Don't kill them. Don't kill them."

She came back with a damp cloth to put over my eyes. I heard sirens. "Ashtyn what's happening."

She sat beside me, rubbing my back, "I have an app. One punch Slider comes, two punches Slider and police come, three punches, well I never punched it three times before. Slider must have been with his riding group because there are maybe a dozen motorcycles, two police cars, and now an ambulance."

I was starting to be able to keep my eyes open, "But you saved me before any of them showed up?"

She laughed, "A girl should never go out without her pepper spray. Unfortunately, you were really close to that guy who was holding you, so you got some spray also."

The ambulance guy came and got me. Ashtyn followed us to the back of the ambulance. They were the same team as when I was in the car wreck and when I had my ruptured appendix. They had me lay down. They flushed my eyes with a saline solution, it stung at first and then was better. He said, "They'll wash them out again at the Hospital."

I sat up, "I'm not going to the Hospital."

Slider was there then and said, "Yes, you are."

I decided if he thought I should go, I should go. The police officer came to the back of the ambulance, "I'll come to the hospital to take a statement." I had calmed down internally. I wasn't sure whether I would press charges or not.

When the policeman left, the ambulance tech turned to Ashtyn, "I guess you're his sister and need to ride with him?"

Ashtyn smiled and climbed up into the ambulance.

Time for this One to Go Home

Ashtyn stayed with me in the ER, she was beside me holding onto my hand, I think now that everything had calmed down, she was scared about what could have happened. Dr. Amm came into my little area, "Perry, Perry, what have you done now?"

I was sitting up, "I'm okay, Dr. Amm. I got mugged, but Ashtyn took them down with her pepper spray." I didn't feel okay. I was still scared.

Dr. Amm said, "Good job, young lady." She took my hand, "Does it hurt?"

I was honest, "Just a little and my eyes are stinging less."

She said, "Look at these hematomas starting to show. That's the medical term for bruises, I say that so you think I went to medical school, but really I just did very well on SAT vocabulary. You were seriously manhandled. The police will want photos, and I want an x-ray. We should check your ribs also, and we'll want to wash out your eyes."

She left, and Slider's girlfriend, Nurse Holly, showed up in civilian clothes. Ashtyn melted into her arms and started crying.

I told her, "Ashtyn saved me. She peppered sprayed those two thugs; she was amazing."

The policeman came, he said he wanted to talk to Ashtyn after he talked to me. Holly and Ashtyn went out to the waiting area. The officer explained it wasn't a matter of me pressing charges. They would be charged with assault whether I said anything or not. I told him about the original encounter and then what happened today. He didn't know anything about what happened to my pool cue. After he left, they came and washed out my eyes again and then took me off to x-ray. After x-ray, I was left in this cold dark hall. No one was waiting to go in, and no one came for me. I was dozing. I had the pool cue in my hand. I was fiercely beating something. I heard someone screaming, it was me. I kept pounding the heavy end of the pool cue into the ground or into Skull's head. I felt wet on my cheeks. I thought it must be blood. When Holly and Ashtyn arrived, I was laying on my back screaming.

Holly started stroking my arm, Ashtyn was holding my other hand. Holly said, "You're having a panic attack. You're okay. You're safe. Everything is good." She touched my face wiping away my tears. The transfer person showed up, and they walked with me back to ER. I needed to go home.

I told Holly, "I need to go home. I need to go home, now. I need my phone. I don't have my phone."

Holly pulled out her phone, "What's your dad's number?" I didn't know it, I didn't know my mother's either. "Do your parents have a landline?" Again no.

I said, "Ashtyn, call Cam. She has their numbers, but don't tell her why."

She looked at me like it was impossible, she called, "Cam, I need you to trust me. I need Perry's dad's phone number. I just need it." Cam finally gave it.

Ashtyn dialed the phone and gave it to me, "Dad, it's Perry. I don't know where my phone is, I'm at the Emergency Room at the Hospital, I need you to come get me. I'm okay, I need you to take me home. Don't tell anyone where I am. I need to get home." I gave her back the phone.

Holly asked, "Do you want me to ask Dr. Amm about some medicine?"

That made me shake, "No, I just need to go home. I need to go home."

They showed up to take pictures of the bruising on my arm and my chest. When they finished, I got off the bed and pulled off the hospital gown. I was standing there in front of Ashtyn and Holly in nothing but my underwear. I could have been naked I wouldn't have cared. I found the bag with my clothes and started getting dressed. Holly said, "The Doctor needs to release you."

I said, "I need to go home."

Holly said, "Perry, tell me what's happening. What are you feeling?"

She was speaking slowly and gently like they do in the old movies right before they pull out the restraints and take the crazy person away. "I feel unsafe. I'm not safe here." I turned to her. I realized I'd cocked my head to the left, turning Blotch away from people. It had been months since I did tht. I was aware of every noise. There were hundreds of machines each making a little noise. Holly whispered something to Ashtyn who left. I told Holly, "I know what I'm feeling isn't right, but if I can get home, I'll be okay. I just need to get home. I need to be in my room, in my room."

"Okay, why don't you lay back down until your dad comes, and then I'm sure you can leave."

I don't know when I started, but I was pacing, up and down my little ER room. Dr. Amm showed up followed by a nurse and Ashtyn. I said, "I'm okay. I don't need anything. I only need to go home. I don't know why no one can see that."

Dr. Amm sat down. Holly left and took Ashtyn with her, the other nurse stepped back. I said, "I know you are trying to de-escalate the situation, but I'm not escalated. I'm not escalated. I'm not safe, and I want to be in my room. I need to be in my room."

Dr. Amm said, "Perry, all I ever want is what is best for you. I've done all the paperwork, and you can go if you want to. If you want to stay here until you feel safe, that can also happen."

I said, "Thank you, Dr. Amm. I'm going to go; I need to go." The nurse gave me some papers to sign. I walked out.

Holly and Ashtyn stepped in beside me, "Perry let us stay with you until your dad comes."

I was still walking, "If he's not here, I'll go ahead and walk home."

She was resting a hand on my arm, "I can drive you; no need to walk."

When we went out the door, Dad drove up, I turned and said, "See I'm all good, all good. I'm going to my room." I climbed in Dad's car, and we left.

Dad wanted me to tell him what happened, but I couldn't. I laid my head back and closed my eyes. I answered everything he said with, "I need to be home." As soon as he pulled into the driveway and stopped the car, I ran into the house. I went to my room, closed all my blinds and drapes, put on pajama pants and a t-shirt, and crawled under all my covers. When my parents came, I said, "I can't talk now. I'll talk later."

An Appearance

I guess I got home from the ER around two I came out of my room at five and found my parents sitting in the den. Mom said, "We talked to Dr. Amm and Slider. Are you okay?"

I sat down, "I'm fine, nothing broken, except the pool cue. I'm bruised. I lost my phone."

Dad said, "Slider brought by your phone."

I said, "I left my Jeep at the Mall."

Dad said, "Slider took me to get it."

I didn't care, "I've made some decisions. I want to go back to homeschooling. You were right; I don't belong out there. I want you to see if there is a way to finish this semester from home, and then we'll re-enroll in the online school."

Mom asked, "What about the fundraiser?"

"I don't know? I don't know? I can't do it," I went back to my room. I came out to get food. I ate in my room. I came out to use the bathroom. I got a jar with a lid so that I didn't have to go out to pee every time. I was safe. I kept my dresser in front of the door while I was in the room. Someone came to my door, knocked, and spoke. I don't know who.

Every time I came out of my room, Mom or Dad was there waiting for me. The conversations went something like this.

"Tell us what you are feeling. It will be good to talk about it."

"I can't."

"It will feel better if you do."

"I need time."

"Dr. Amm and Dr. Pender talked. They sent over some pills; they'll help."

I took the pills. I faked swallowing. I spit them out as soon as I left the room.

"We love you. Your friends are worried about you."

"I need time."

"Take another pill."

"I need time." I slept.

Things, I know, went on while I was in my room. My best guess of how they went:

The first phone call between Mom and Cam.

Mom: Cam, please help.

Cam: It sounds like you won. You have him right where you wanted him.

Mom: Cam what does that mean?

Cam: You didn't want him playing pool. You wanted him homeschooled. It took him getting mugged, but you got what you wanted. You win.

Mom, Tears, Hang up.

The second phone call between Mom and Cam.

Mom: Cam, please help.
Cam: I'm sorry for what I said.
Mom: No, I deserved it. I got what I wanted, and I was wrong. The life has gone out of him. I want the Perry that loved you and loved life and couldn't imagine not being able to raise forty thousand dollars.
Cam: I don't know where that Perry went.
Mom: He turns his face to the left as he talks to us. He hasn't done that in months. Please help.
Cam: I'll help.

Maybe it was Sunday afternoon when I came out to look for food, I put two slices of lunchmeat, a plastic wrapped cheese and some mayonnaise on a plate and headed to my room. Instead of my parents, Cam was in the den, when I went back through. Maybe she was there the first time, and I didn't see her. She stood, I said in a gentle, quiet way, "I can't. Not yet. I need time." I went on to my room. I'm not even sure what I meant.

Josh was there waiting for me once. It went about the same as it had with Cam. He was crying as I left him.

More stuff that went on:

Call to Mom's therapist.
Call to Tristan's therapist; he specializes in teenage boys.

Call to Dr. Pender.

Call to Dr. Amm.

Discussion of taking my room by force.

Discussion of blocking my return to my room.

Discussion of taking me to the hospital by force.

Discussion of having a group intervention, with everyone waiting in the den for me to come out of my room.

Monday morning, Mom knocked. Through the door, she asked, "Will you be okay if we go to work?"

From beneath my covers, I called out, "I'll be okay."

Mom took this as a breakthrough, so she texted Cam, 'I think he's better; someone come over this afternoon. Maybe he's ready.'

My friends gathered at lunch on Monday and discussed next moves. At three-thirty, my door started opening, and my dresser started moving. I sat up in my bed and watched. My room was dark, and there was no light in the hallway. When the door was all the way open, I still couldn't see who it was. I couldn't even place the body shape or size.

They came in and sat at my desk. I asked, "Who are you?"

He said, "Once, I was having a bad day and bemoaning how good everyone else had it when this guy got up in my face with how we all have some problem. I hardly knew him, and he was all up on me.

"Do you think Ashtyn isn't scared to death? Slider brought her to school today. When you didn't show, she got scared. She called Slider to take her home. You don't think Gene didn't scare the shit out of Sean, and do you think Sean doesn't always have to look over his shoulder to make sure he's safe? Do you think Gene hasn't lost friends because he's dating Ashtyn? He got Darden back, but people say things behind his back and to his face. Almost every woman is aware, if not scared when she walks across a parking lot in the dark. You don't think I've heard people say 'fag' behind my back? So this guy was all up in my face, and he got me started on the path of realizing I had more decisions than I did problems. Do you know I love that guy? And I'm not going to sit by while he hides in the dark and morphs into a giant cockroach."

I was sitting on the side of my bed now. "Thanks, Rick. I'm scared, and I don't like that feeling. I once told Cam the scars and bruises tell me I'm alive. This overwhelmed me." We sat in silence, "How did you get in?"

He said, "Apparently everyone knows where your spare key is hidden."

I asked, "How come you came?"

He laughed, "Everyone wanted to come, but it got down to Cam and me. Everyone thought it needed to be someone you didn't expect and if it didn't work, I was going to use Cam's Plan B to get you out of bed."

"What was Plan B?"

He said, "Crawling into bed with you."

I said, "I think that is so politically incorrect."

He laughed, "Okay enough of this. You told everyone you needed time. Time's up. You stink! When was the last time you showered?"

I said, "Friday."
He shook his head, "Then hit the shower."

While I was in the shower, he came in the bathroom and got my bed clothes and left clean clothes. When I got to my room, he had stripped the sheets off my bed and gathered up the dirty clothes and dishes from the floor. "What are you doing?"

He started opening the drapes and blinds, "We are putting life back into your room."

Before I could stop him, he opened the window. The alarm was ear piercing. Did I mention we have an alarm system? No, I didn't, because we never think about it unless we're going out of town. However, the windows are always on. I ran to the code box. I typed in 0409, my birthdate. Mom came in the door right then. She asked, "Are you escaping?" Then she realized I had showered and changed clothes. I could see her trying to find the right words to not scare me back into the cave.

I hugged her, "I'm glad you and Dad are my parents, I needed this time." Rick came up behind me, "Mom, this is Rick. The lunch table sent him over to get me out of bed."

Rick put out his hand, and Mom took it, "Hi Ms. Larcon, I rinsed his dirty dishes and put them in the dishwasher. I hope that is right, and now I'm looking for clean sheets for his bed and can we leave the window open for a while. The room needs airing out."

"Oh, I love you." She hugged him. "Follow me, and I'll get you the sheets."

When he got back to my room, he saw the Honeysuckle Candle Cam had given me. He lit it then picked up the jar of piss that was sitting next to it. He said, "I don't want to know what this is, I don't ever want to talk about it again, and I want it to go away." He handed it to me. I poured the contents into the toilet and took the jar to the kitchen. Mom said, "Throw that jar away. Do not put it in recycling." When I got back, he was making my bed, I sat watching him. He asked, "Are you ready to turn on your phone yet?"

I looked around for it, "No."

He put a nurse's corner on the top sheet, "Then you finish this and let me send out some texts."

I did as I was told. I couldn't imagine questioning his instructions. He started walking out of the room while texting. I asked, "Where are you going?"

He said, "To tell your mom you invited me to stay for dinner." I hadn't invited him, but again I couldn't imagine disagreeing with him.

It's About The Blotch

Before we headed to supper, he sat me down. "I need to say some things." I was a little taken aback by his forcefulness, but I sat. He continued. "I've heard the whole discussion about Vision Leader, and I think it's B.S. I'm here because of the power of Blotch. No, not Josh's Blotch guilt joke. I'm here because every day, everywhere you go, you can't stop saying I am Blotch, and you do it boldly and proudly. I'm working to be as strong as you. I want to be brave enough to wear a T-shirt that proclaims Equality or says 'I'm Gay' or 'I'm Gay for Jesse.' And one last thing, you've been turning your face to the left, and you've been doing it since I got here. Cam said you better stop it before she sees you."

I stood up and hugged him.

Supper was meatloaf, green beans, mashed potatoes, and salad. Rick acted like it was the best meal he ever had. Conversation tiptoed around me, they didn't even tell the story of my conception. They focused on Rick. He was usually reclusive at the lunch table, but he was coming out of his shell for my parents. At some point toward the end of eating, I realized it was Monday, and there was the mixer. Remember, Cam, set up a mixer at the coffee shop as a thank you to the volunteers? I started hyperventilating. Everything went black, a shaking beginning deep at my core and started moving out. I could feel sweat beginning to bead up on my skin. In my mind, like a dream, I was clawing my way back to my room. There were hands rubbing my shoulders. Rick said, "As I count to five slowly, breathe in. As I count again, slowly breathe out. You're in a safe place. Let's do it again. You're in a good place, and now one more time. Now tell us what scared you?"

I said, "I can't stand up in front of all those people and talk."

He was still rubbing my shoulders, "Can you imagine talking to them each individually? Could you mill around and talk to everyone?"

I said, "Yeah, I can do that."

He went and sat back down. I was amazed at this whole afternoon. This guy who barely spoke was putting me back together. I sat for a few moments just looking at my plate. The attack had drained me. Mom, Dad, and Rick may have been talking. When I came out of my funk, I turned to my dad, "Dad could Rick borrow a shirt from your closet, maybe even a sports coat? I think they would fit, don't you?"

Dad looked at me and then Rick, "Rick do you suddenly have a date or something?"

"Not that I'm aware of."

I said, "He's the spokesperson for the Big Hustle, and we want him to look nice when he takes the stage tonight."

Rick started to object. I said, "I can't imagine going if I can't be sure I won't be asked to speak to the whole crowd. I can't." My hand holding my fork started trembling. Everyone stared at it. I flattened it against the table to make it stop.

Rick reluctantly agreed. After supper, Mom took him back to Dad's closet, and picked out a shirt, a jacket, and even a tie. She worked with his hair. The transformation was amazing. He was holding his head up and standing up straight. He was confident. It was time to go. As we were leaving my room, I reached for my keys. He put his hand on top of them and said, "No, Demetri will be here in a minute to pick us up. Josh and Cam will bring you home whenever you are ready to leave."

Please Send Perry Forty Thousand Dollars

Not only Ashtyn, but all my friends were working together to save me. Before I had physical traumas, and my body needed to recoup. This time I had a psychological trauma, and I had needed rest to recoup. As I rode in Demetri's car, there was still fear in me. I kept saying in my head, 'you are safe.' Rick had his hand on my arm; it felt good. It was what Josh would have done if he were there. The coffee shop was packed. In fact, a lot of people were standing outside talking. Emile had been texting as we drove over, so I wasn't surprised that Cam was waiting for me. She took my arm and held on to me as I began to greet and thank people. We worked our way around the outside people and then went in. Josh brought me a decaf ice coffee, and someone came up and offered me a brownie, I turned to Cam almost crying. "You made brownies without me?"

She said, "We didn't have a choice."

"You're not mad at me for going off the grid."

She said, "I knew where you were the whole time, and I could watch you through the webcam."

I looked at her, "You could not."

She only smiled. I thought about how Josh had been on my computer the last time he slept over. I needed to check this out. People knew I had been mugged at the mall, but only the lunch table knew I had a total panic meltdown and had been in hibernation for forty-eight hours, so there was not a lot of 'I'm glad you're better.'

Sean was there with Letty who was now his girlfriend. She was sparky and delightful.

When Cam needed to go brief Rick on some spokesperson things, Josh took her place. He stood right beside me, my left arm straight down my side, my fingers interlocked with the fingers of his right hand. It was very calming. I don't know how he knew exactly what I needed.

Josh whispered in my ear, "So did Rick have to climb into bed with you?"

I told him, "No, but I think he wanted to."

He laughed, "Yeah, everyone wants Perry. Who did the makeover on him?"

I said, "My mother. Isn't it something?"

I let go of Josh long enough to hug Letty.

We kept circulating. At a quarter of eight, Rick took the mic.

"Hi, I'm Rick, and an hour ago I was volunteered as the spoke person for the Big Hustle. So first a big round of applause for all of you because you are doing a fabulous job." Applause and hollering. "Our identifiable income at this time can be estimated at $25,000, and our Leadership Team thinks there are a couple of more avenues of income that will get us to our forty thousand dollar goal. I hope all of you have been on the website to see the video tour of the Renaissance Center. Pah is a great guy, and that tour is great, so you know how important what we are doing is. Everyone has done so much I hate to ask, but there is one more small favor. If you are eating at Billiard and Burgers, thank them for hosting the Big Hustle and, if you are shopping at any store in the Mall, thank them for donating to the Big Hustle silent auction. At this point, ninety percent of the stores have donated. Thank you, ladies. We're no longer calling you the mean girls; you are now the shopping girls." The girls hollered up a storm. "And a big thanks to Henry for his advice, counsel and coffee shop. Now, finally, we have a few things for Perry our Vision Leader." Every one applauded. I raised my hand. Josh was still beside me holding tightly to my hand. My heart started racing. He must have known because he brought his other hand over to pat my arm.

Cam took the stage. Looking at me she said, "We were going to save this as a surprise for the day of the Big Hustle, but we decided it made more sense to share it with you and with everyone else tonight. Perry's pool cue got broken over the weekend, and he has been desperate to know where it is. Someone quickly gathered it up on Saturday, some phone calls were made, and Saturday afternoon it was sent by air express to the McDerman Pool Cue Factory to be made whole. We expect it back in plenty of time for the Big Hustle." Applause. "In the meantime, we received from Minnesota today, this new cue that is as close as possible in size and weight to your cue. It's yours to practice with and keep." Everyone applauded.

Cam came down and joined Josh and me. As Cam handed me my new cue, I asked Cam, "How did all that come about?"

She said, "The manager at the sporting goods store did it all."

I said, "You are so lying."

And as you can guess, she said, "That's my story, and I'm sticking to it."

Rick was back on stage and had everyone's attention. "You all are doing amazing things, but we are not giving a prize for who raises the most money or volunteers the most. What we hope is that you have new experiences, learn some skills and grow. A big thanks to the people in the entrepreneurial club for their training videos, which by the way have been entered into a competition and are advancing to the semi-finals." Applause. "Now I want to share with you my favorite video and my favorite fundraiser, a new internet superstar at over ten thousand views." The coffee shop was not a sports bar, so it only had one small TV, so a large screen had been brought in.

From across the room in a very excited voice, Marlin shouted out, "Perry, this is me! This is me! I love you, Perry!"

Marlin came on the screen with his two moms beside him, "My name is Marlin, I'm not supposed to tell you my last name, I attend school at the Renaissance Center. I'm here because my friend Perry (As he said my name he signed U blotch R) needs your help. He needs forty thousand dollars. If he doesn't get it by May thirty-first, the Renaissance Center will close, and Perry won't be able to tutor me in math, and he will be despondent. So please send Perry forty thousand dollars to save my school, and so he can tutor me." One of his mothers leaned over to whisper in his ear. He added, "If you don't have all forty thousand, please send some money." Everyone cheered and applauded. I teared up. The words on paper don't convey the sincerity, innocence, and authenticity of Marlin's request. He saw none of it as being about him, just his school and me. Pictures of the school, me, and the Fundsup page had appeared at different times in the video.

Rick got on stage to wrap things up, and I had Cam help me work through the crowd to Marlin and his mothers. I asked if I could hug him, and he said yes. He started getting way too excited. His moms helped him put on sound deadening earphones, and we walked them out. I wanted to ask them about Sadie and the man in the park, but I didn't know what to ask. As Cam and I hugged his mothers, they said, "We didn't even know your name, other than the sign for you, until a month ago. Thank you for what you're doing. Both of our employers signed on as sponsors." They both kissed me.

On our way home, I said, "You all are amazing. Why don't I know about these videos and the additional training videos? And the Fundsup page?"

Josh said, "I've limited your computer to only some information about the Big Hustle."

"You blocked me? Why?"

Cam leaned in close to me, "Perry, we are doing this for the center, but we are also doing this for you, and we want there to be some surprises like tonight."

I exclaimed, "I forgot my pool cue."

Shannon said, "I got it; it's in the trunk."

I said to Cam, "How did all that really happen?"

Cam said, "Slider picked up the pool cue and your phone so that they wouldn't end up forever in some police evidence locker. Then the guy from sporting goods came by and said let me take care of that."

I said, "You know, I know you are lying."

As we drove up to my house, Cam whispered in my ear, "I'm going to walk you to the door." As we got out of the car, she said to Josh, "You don't need to wait; I'm spending the night." We got the cue out of the trunk. As we walked to the door, she whispered to me, "Rick did put clean sheets on your bed?" My face was a sunrise city on a two sun planet. At the door, she whispered, "I'm so glad you are back. I really do want a webcam, so I can watch you sleep." We kissed. Words are inadequate for how good and safe I felt in her arms at that moment. Cam wasn't really spending the night.

Inside I sat down with my parents. "I am okay. I was scared, and I needed those forty-eight hours. I needed the space, and I needed Rick coming over today. And, I need the two of you."

Dad said, "Your friends are going to drive you everywhere you need to go this week. You haven't lost your car privileges. They offered to do it, and we think it's a good idea."

I told them, "Somewhere they became experts on panic attacks. Could you believe Rick at supper tonight? I was about to come apart, and he walked me back from the edge."

My mother said, "We're glad you're back, and we're going to do all we can to keep you away from the edge. Now, my answer is no to homeschooling and no to quitting the fundraiser." Smiling she said, "I'm serious."

Dad added, "Also we talked, and we're going to cancel our retreat. We'll do it some other time."

I insisted, "No, don't do that. I'll be fine. At least wait and see how this week goes." They agreed. I was torn about them going. As I had told Mom, I'm sixteen, but I've never been unable to call them since I got a phone. They were always just a few numbers away. Even when I turned off my phone, I knew I could turn it back on and call.

You Will Never Be Alone

I woke up in the night screaming. I was sitting up in my bed when my dad turned on my light. He sat down beside me putting a hand on my shoulder. He quietly said, "You're safe. You're safe. We're going to keep you safe. Your friends are going to keep you safe."

I leaned against him, "I don't even remember what I was dreaming, but I'm okay."

Dad said, "I'm going to leave the hall light on."

I asked, "Like a night light?"

I love my dad. He said, "No Perry, as a night light."

I smiled as I lay back down. Grammar lessons taught in the middle of the night. I heard Dad sit down on the stairs. I called out, "Dad, I'm okay. Go back to bed." I heard him get up.

Josh and Cam came to pick me up at 7:10. I told them, "I need what you're doing. I'm not going to lie. I had a nightmare last night. I woke up screaming; there is still a lot of scared in me."

Cam said, "We're ready for anything, Perry. Not just the table, a select few others are ready. Believe me, you are never going to be alone. There will always be someone near."

I shook, "That is scary."

Josh said, "Perry, this is about people you have given to, giving back."

I had to ask, "How did everyone become such an expert on taking care of people with panic attacks? Last night at dinner, I started falling apart at the thought of facing all those people, and in a second Rick was behind me rubbing my shoulders and telling me to breathe."

Cam said, "Ashtyn told us about what happened at the hospital, so we went online and learned about panic attacks."

I asked, "Is Ashtyn okay? I didn't get to talk to her last night."

Cam said, "She was left scared, cautious and shaken, but she's doing okay. She came with Gene last night."

We were at school. More to myself than to Cam or Josh, I said, "I'm going to be okay. I am." Cam walked to class with me.

The week was uneventful for the most part, and my friends took terrific care of me. As Cam had promised, it seemed there was always someone stepping in beside me to walk with me from one class to the next. Between some classes, it was like a relay. Someone would walk me halfway, and suddenly they would have to turn another direction, but their replacement was right there. I had another nightmare Tuesday night and one panic attack at school. On Thursday in English Lit, I had forgotten the book we were reading from, but I was sure it was in my backpack. As I kept searching, I started hyperventilating and shaking. Then there were hands on my shoulders, and a girl saying, "Breathe in slowly, now let it out slowly, now again." Then from somewhere she laid a copy on my desk and said, "You can use this today. Just don't mark on it because it's a classroom copy." When I was okay, Karalyne went back to her desk and sat down.

Zach, who you don't know, leaned over and said, "If she put her hands on me and told me to breathe slowly, I think I would pass out."

Friday was my first-day-back driving, and I was to pick up Cam and Josh. Everything was one step at a time and, other than the nightmares and the attack Karalyne talked me through, I had been good.

I had waited to see Cam face to face to ask this, Josh was in the back seat Cam was in the front with me. "Karalyne?" I knew she would have heard about English Lit.

Cam pulled out her fingernail board, "She was the only person in that class I trusted to make sure you were okay. She and I have grown closer."

I looked in the rearview mirror at Josh with an 'Are you believing this?' look.

As a big step, I was spending Friday night at Josh's. The four of us were going to family night and then a movie. The nice thing we had worked out was, when the evening was over, Josh drops Cam and me off in front of her house and then takes Shannon home. We could kiss as long as we wanted, and I would walk home to Josh's.

Cam and I sat down on her front steps. I told her, "This morning you said this was people giving back to me, but I want you to know you have given so much to me. I was a mess when we met last September, and I've been a mess most of this year. It's you who has helped me to stand up, hold my head up, and say hello world here I am."

She ran her fingers through my hair, "You did all that, I've just been along for the ride."

I said, "I don't think so," and leaned in for a kiss. I walked home. (My home at Josh's house.)

What Makes a Man

My dad showed up at Josh's at twelve-thirty. It was obvious Josh knew he was coming. Dad asked, "Do you guys want to go shoot some pool?"

Josh turned to me. I looked at the floor. When I raised my head, I said, "Yeah, I guess we ought too."

On the way, Dad asked, "Hey Josh do you know what makes you a man?"

Josh shot back, "I'm guessing a beautiful woman, a hot car, and a wad of cash is not the answer."

I gave him a big smile and a fist bump.

Dad ignored his answer, "A man overcomes his excuses to do what is right, and he also takes responsibility for his actions. You stand up to the bully even though you have a hundred reasons not to. You also do what needs to be done. Sometimes there are unpleasant tasks that you don't want to do, but they need to be done. Telling someone at work, they need to bathe more often or at home unstopping a clogged toilet. In relationships, it's sharing in responsibility, and when you're married and a father, you share in the parenting including changing diapers. Do I need to go on?"

I said, "Thanks, Dad."

At the mall, we parked across from the dumpster enclosure. I don't think Dad even realized what he was doing. He got out of the car and turned toward the Mall entrance. I stood looking at the dumpster enclosure. I pointed, "I enter through there," and started walking toward the dumpsters.

Josh asked, "Are you sure?"

I kept walking, I entered the enclosure. Josh and Dad were behind me, I asked, "Dad, where are those guys?"

I knew he would know, "They were in violation of their parole, so they're being held without bail. The district attorney says they'll offer them a plea of three to five years and if they take it, neither you nor Ashtyn will have to testify."

I walked over to the dumpster. I picked a splinter of wood off the ground, probably a piece of my pool cue. I threw it in. There was a scared and maybe scarred core to my body, but the panic seemed to be gone. I walked over to the buzzer by the restaurant's back door. While we waited to be let in, Dad pulled out his wallet, "Here's twenty bucks. You guys have a good time. If you need a ride home, call."

Joey from the wait staff opened the door. I hugged Dad and then, to my surprise, so did Josh. As we walked through the kitchen, Josh said, "You know he's my dad too."

I'm a lucky son and a lucky brother.

Sunday Night Dinner at Cams

I was at Cam's for dinner Sunday night. We were having pot roast, potatoes, carrots, and green beans. In the middle of dinner, Cam, who had been quiet for most of the evening, said, "Perry thinks the treasurer for the Renaissance Center is embezzling funds, and he plans to confront him at the fundraiser."

I thought 'confront' was a bit strong.

"Why would you think that Perry?" asked Mr. Grant taking a sip of his wine.

I told him what I knew, "The center was supposed to get a grant for twenty-five thousand dollars. The Congressman's office said they did, but Ms. Patel says they didn't. I know Ms. Patel is not lying, and the Congressman's office has no reason to lie."

Putting down his fork, Mr. Grant asked, "Why the treasurer?"

"That is a good question," I told him, "Because they are a small operation, he handles all mail, bank statements, general office work, and creates the financial reports that go to the board."

"That is poor practices but typical of small organizations," he took another sip of wine, "But it doesn't make him guilty. It seems to me you have overlooked one possible route of investigation."

"What did I miss?" I thought I had considered everything.

"You could ask the Congressman's office to verify the check was sent and whether it was cashed. The government is a big place, and there are many places the ball could be dropped. Do you have any connection to the office?"

Cam said, "Sean has spoken to one of his aides."

Mr. Grant said, "Good, call the aide, and ask him to verify the grant check was sent. Don't tell him you suspect anyone, but say there is confusion. Now I understand you were back at the hospital last week."

"I didn't have to stay." I found myself rubbing my right wrist.

"And are you recovered?" He asked.

I told him, "Yes, I had some intense support during the past week, and I feel a hundred percent better now. Thanks for asking."

"I understand the cue is being fixed?" I could tell from his lights, he knew more.

"I believe you would know more about that than I do, sir." I smiled.

He and Cam both smiled. Cam said, "I told you the manager from the sporting goods store was taking care of all that."

I said, "Oh yeah, I forgot. Would you know when I might get it back? The one they sent is very nice, but there is an ever so slight difference between the two."

He smiled, "Of course I'm just guessing, and I know nothing about making pool cues, but probably this coming weekend. There is a daily 3 pm flight from Minneapolis."

I said, "Thank you, sir."

Mrs. Grant said, "Perry you stay seated, and Cam can come help me with dessert."

While they were gone, Mr. Grant said, "I was talking with my guys," (Ashtyn's uncle Slider and his friend Butch work for Cam's dad.) "this week about how much you have been through this year and what you are accomplishing for the center, and we're not surprised you needed a couple of days of rest."

I said, "Thank you, sir. The one good thing that came out of my rest was making Rick spokesperson for the Big Hustle. You should have seen him; he transformed in minutes from a shy guy to take command of the stage. Anyway, it's not about what I have done it's about what over fifty teenage volunteers have done in six weeks time. That is the message I want out there."

"That is a great message."

Is Pops Dead?

After Dinner, we called Sean and got the aide's name and number. I called him on Monday during lunch, and he promised to look into it and get back to me, but it might not be until the Congressman came for the Big Hustle.

It was going to be a quiet week until Ashtyn suggested we thank all the sponsors and donating stores. We decided to follow the model of our gifts to the math class, a bag of small candy bars with a note attached. Instead of the note, we designed small certificates of appreciation. Cam's dad offered to have them printed, so they were sharp and professional looking. Josh had an unfinished basement where we could set up tables to assemble the gifts.

Two hundred stores had donated, and we had almost a hundred business sponsors. We met to assemble the gifts right after school on Thursday, and as soon as we could, we started sending teams out with a dozen at a time to the sponsoring businesses. The mall map was in color-coded sections, so we used that to assign teams to the mall for delivery and to prevent overlap. We also decided it would be easier to just thank all the stores in the mall, even the ones that hadn't donated.

I was saying my thank yous and working the details. The man, not Marlin's Dad, had to be happy.

My parents left Friday afternoon for their couples retreat. I was bummed about the fact I would be unable to contact them from the time they checked in Friday afternoon until sometime Sunday afternoon when it ended. I told them I was fine.

I went to Josh's for the weekend.

We went to family and friends at the Banners. I didn't go in the bathroom once.

Nothing exciting happened Saturday. I went and practiced at the restaurant in the morning, and Josh went with me. Late afternoon, we had set aside an hour to work on math. We were finishing up when Nanna called.

Nanna: Perry, where are your parents? I've been calling all afternoon.

She was trying to sound casual, but I knew something was wrong.

Me: Nanna, what's the matter.

Nanna: I just need to speak to your parents.

Me: They're at a retreat and can't be reached until Sunday afternoon.

Nanna: Who is looking after you?

Me: I'm at my friend Josh's house. Tell me what has happened.

Nanna: Now do as I tell you and take the phone to one of his parents. No more questions.

I took the phone to Mrs. Benton. She walked outside with it. Mr. Benton looked at me. I told him, "It's my Nanna; she wouldn't tell me what it was about." He got up and followed his wife outside. Josh had joined me by this point, and we watched through the kitchen window. Mrs. Benton gave the phone to her husband, he talked to Nanna for a while and then hung up. They stood in the driveway talking for ten minutes, before checking something on Mr. Benton's phone. A heavy weight was sinking in my gut. I told Josh, "Pops is dead." I fell into one of the chairs at the breakfast table. Josh was silent. It made me think he thought it too.

I waited for them to return. They came in and sat down. Mr. Benton said, "Breathe in slowly, Perry. It's not that bad. Now breathe out slowly. Your Pops had a mild heart attack. He's doing fine now, but he's asking for you."

I jumped up to get my keys. I came back with my keys; I was ready to run out the door and drive to Philly. Mrs. Benton got up, and while steering me back to my seat, said, "We are going to send you to see him, but we're not going to let you drive."

Mr. Benton said, "We have booked you and Josh on the 8 a.m. train for Philadelphia, and you can come home in the afternoon on the 3:30 train. Now call your Nanna, tell her the plan, and let her tell you what has happened."

I called her back. Pop had a small heart attack. They put in some things that expand the arteries, and he should be home in a few days. When I tried to tell her when we would arrive, I couldn't remember the times. I couldn't even repeat them correctly when they told them to me. She reassured me that Pop was alright.

After talking to Nanna, I told the Bentons, "My dad said I'm not allowed to leave the state without permission."

Mr. Benton said, "We are giving you permission. I'm sure your parents will approve."

Josh and I went back to our room. I was a mess. I didn't cry. I tried to shut everything out. But after fifteen minutes of me flopping around the room from computer, to earbuds, to my bed, Josh said, "Go run or walk it off. You need to go."

I headed out. I had about an hour and a half of sunlight left, so I headed to Green Lake Park. I stood for a while just looking at the lake before taking the trail. Instead of our usual going to the right, I went to the left. I guess it didn't make a difference, but before I had always gone to the right. Slowly the fear began to leave me. It was replaced by the excitement of the adventure and getting to see Nanna and Pops. I was feeling good when I came to the field with the man and Sadie playing Frisbee.

Sadie caught the Frisbee and brought it to me. The man followed. Expecting to be chastised for something, I said indignantly, "What is it today?"

He took the Frisbee; he even had a small smile, "You've done good kid. Your parents are good, and they're proud of what you're doing. The fundraiser is on target. This is probably it. I'm going." He took the Frisbee and turned away.

I grabbed his arm, "But who are you?" I froze as a giant aura encircled him filling all my vision. I heard the music the angels hear; the music that creates and sustains all things. When I let go of him it was gone. He said, "Your Pops is going to be okay." He and Sadie trotted away.

I headed to Cam's house. When she answered the door, I asked if we could sit with Showey in the backyard. We sat in silence. She spoke first, "I heard. Josh called Shannon. I'm sorry."

I said, "He's going to be okay."

"Are you sure?"

I told her, "The guy in the park said so."

"How does he know?" she asked.

I said, "He's an angel, or he was, I think he left."

"What?"

I told her, "I grabbed his arm. His aura filled my vision. It was blinding, and I heard the music the angels hear."

"The music?"

We were sitting close, "As they were freeing me from the car wreck and everyone was singing 'Gloria in Excelsis Deo,' I heard the song of the stars and the planets, the song that sustains and creates, and I heard it again in the park today."

"You never told me."

I smiled, "I didn't want you to think I was weird."

"You thought that would make me think you're weird? It's nothing compared to you constantly hiding in bathrooms."

I leaned in and kissed her.

We sat in silence, she asked, "Are you still going to Philadelphia? I mean if Pops is okay?"

I said, "I get your point, but I need to go because sometime he won't be okay, and I might not make it in time. And he doesn't know he'll be okay, and he wants to see me."

She touched my hair. We kissed, not a passionate kiss but a compassionate kiss. Then I leaned my head beside her, and we hugged. I didn't know there were so many types of kisses until I kissed Cam.

Bad Girls Looking for Bad Boys

Mr. Benton dropped Josh and me off in front of Union Station in Washington D.C. at seven thirty on Sunday morning. We were on our own. We had to call as soon as we were settled on the train and then when we arrived at the hospital in Philly. We were impressed with our independence. We each had a backpack with snacks and water. I had my camera. We had tickets we had printed off at home.

We found the waiting area for our train. This was smooth sailing. At ten until eight, they opened the doors, and we went down to the train platform. We had no trouble finding seats and settling in. Josh called his dad. Right on time, the train pulled out of the station.

There are some great views from the train as we headed north, but as it went through DC and each of the cities, it was like you were driving through the alleys, and the sights were a lot of trash. The seat in front of us faced us, but in the seat after it were two girls who were giggling and trying to get our attention. They would hold their little makeup mirrors up over the seat or around the side of the seat to look at us. They threw some little bits of paper at us.

My phone messaged with a blocked number. 'Where are you going?'

Josh and I puzzled over how they could have gotten my number. Josh thought maybe they hacked my Bluetooth. I messaged back. 'Philadelphia. You?'

Message: 'Same. How old are you?'

Josh and I agreed. 'Seventeen.' That set off quite a giggle storm. You know we're only sixteen.

I texted. 'How old are you?'

Message back. 'Rude question.'

Another message. 'We're looking for bad boys.'

I texted. 'How bad?'

Them. 'Bad enough.'

I texted. 'Why don't you join us and find out if we're bad enough?'

More giggles. With this much giggling, how old could they be? They were getting up. As soon as they turned around, Josh punched me in the arm and said, "I told you it was Cam and Shannon." He hadn't said that.

Shannon said, "Oh you so did not know, and the two of you were flirting with total strangers."

Cam said, "And lying saying you were seventeen."

I said, "Can you blame a guy for trying?"

Josh asked, "What are you doing here?"

Shannon said, "Did you two think we were going to let you go on this trip unsupervised. Your parents hired us to make sure you didn't fall under the spell of any bad girls."

Josh laughed, "That is so not true."

Cam settled in beside me, "I wanted to make sure you were okay. Are you okay?"

I told her, "I couldn't be better."

We got to Philadelphia just after ten. We had checked the location of the hospital, and it was only ten blocks. Even though we knew where we were going, I insisted we go to the visitor's information desk. The lady told us which door to go out of and showed us that the Liberty Bell and Independence Hall were all near the hospital. When we got clear of the station, we crossed a bridge into what I guessed was downtown Philly. We were on quieter streets now. Cam asked, "Why'd you ask about all those other things? Aren't you here to see Pops?"

"Mrs. Benton said I shouldn't stay more than fifteen or twenty minutes with Pops. So the plan is we will go visit, and I'll ask Nanna if she wants to go to lunch with us. We'll do lunch and some other things, and then I'll go back at two to visit again, before we head for the three thirty train."

She laughed, "A man with a plan. Don't be scared."

"I'm trying not to be."

She held tightly to my arm, "The man in the park said he would be okay."

"I know, but those angels can be temperamental, and he definitely wasn't the nicest angel I ever heard of." The walk took an hour because I kept making Cam and Shannon pose for pictures in front of interesting things. Sometimes they draped over Josh like he was a model or a star. Have I ever told you my brother is pretty good looking?

When we came in sight of the hospital, I froze for a minute. Everyone stopped and looked at me. Cam rubbed my arm. I said, "It's so real."

Josh was on my other side, "This is not about a hospital or being sick or anything. This is about seeing Pops."

The Visit

I started walking. Inside, I made it inside. I went to the information desk. The man there told me Pop was in the Cardiac Care Unit (CCU). We had to go to a particular waiting room and call in to be admitted. When we got there, Cam sat me down and looked me in the face. "I know you've been in ICU, but it's different when you're the visitor. There are going to be machines with his heartbeat and all kinds of other information. He may have some IV's and other tubes; don't look at any of that. Look at Pops. He may be pale or grey, just remember you have looked worse and lived. If he can't talk, you talk. Tell him about the train ride, the Big Hustle, your fabulous girlfriend." I laughed.

While Cam was preparing me, Josh got on the phone saying he was me and asking for admission. Nanna showed up and hugged everyone. "Thank you all for coming. You can't all come in, but Pop will be glad to know you all came with Perry." She looked at me, "Come on, Perry. It's going to be okay." As we walked into CCU Nanna took my arm, "Pops fell when he had the heart attack, and he has a bruise on the side of his face. It's not as bad as it looks. I looked around for Nurse Kelly, but I knew this wasn't that hospital. A nurse smiled at me.

Pops was in a separate little room with a glass wall just like the ICU I had been in. I stood by the bed; he didn't look so good, pale or even grey except for the bruise that covered the whole left side of his face. It made me cringe. My eyes filled with tears. Nanna touched his hand. She said, "Pops, Perry is here."

He opened his eyes, a tear rolled down my cheek. For the first time, Pop looked old. He spoke with a whispery voice, "Why are you crying?"

"You cried when I was in the hospital."

He had a quiet laugh, "You looked really bad."

I said, "You've looked better. Do you hurt?"

"No, I'm going to be okay."

I said, "I know you are." More tears rolled down my face.

"Eventually there will be a time when I won't be."

I told him, "I know that too. You better take better care of yourself."

"Nanna's already rearranging all our food plans. Thank you for coming."

I told him, "When I was in the hospital, Cam would lay down in the bed beside me."

He laughed quietly again, "I bet that was nice."

"If you didn't have so many tubes and wires, I would lay down beside you here."

"I would like that. When you were little, I would lay down with you at nap time until you fell asleep. A couple of times, I fell asleep before you, and you got up to play. Nanna would be so mad at me because, without a nap, you would be cranky the rest of the day."

I said, "I love you, Pops."

He fell asleep.

Nanna hugged me, "You don't know how good this is for him. You brought him some life energy." I kept hugging her for a while.

I asked, "Do you want to go to lunch with us?"

She said, "The hospital brings me lunch, and I haven't seen his doctor yet today, so I need to stay."

"I'll be back around two."

She said, "I love you, Perry."

One of the nurses followed me out, she touched me on the shoulder, and I turned around, "I just wanted to tell you that meant everything to your grandfather and not everyone your age is brave enough to come in here."

I said, "Thanks." She hugged me.

I found Cam alone in the waiting room. I guess I looked surprised. She said, "We thought you might need some space to decompress. Are you okay?"

"I told him when I was in the hospital, you would lay beside in the bed and that I wanted to lay down beside him, but there were too many tubes and wires."

She said, "That's beautiful."

We sat for a few minutes.

In the lobby, I asked about a place for lunch. The guy at the information desk said the sports bar in the hotel next to the hospital had some of the best sandwiches in Philly and that it was early enough to where it wouldn't be crowded yet. We headed next door. As we walked in, I noticed Josh, Cam, and Shannon were acting a little weird, but I was still too bummed to care.

We got a table. There were televisions on every wall. More than at Burgers and Billiards. I couldn't count the total number, and they were all showing different games. To one side there were some pool tables. The waitress took our order. (I know you don't care, but I got a Rueben. It's my favorite, not at home sandwich.) I saw our waitress make the sign 'U-Blotch-R' to one of the other waitresses. The second waitress came around to bring us water even though we hadn't asked for it. When she left, I said, "The first waitress told the waitress who brought the water, 'U-Blotch-R' and pointed at me."

They all three looked around, Josh said, "Maybe you're imagining things."

I said, "I love you brother, but your lights tell me you're lying, and somewhere on me I have a can of whup-ass I'm going to open up on you if you don't start talking." They all three cracked up. I said, "What?"

Cam said, "You talking all tough is hilarious. Here is the scoop. The McDerman Company is staging seven additional fundraisers across the country hosted by members of their champion tournament team, each benefiting a local spectrum center in their community. This happens to be one of the host places. There were posters by the door we kept you from seeing."

I got up and went back to the door. There were posters featuring me. When I came back to the table, the waitress was just leaving. She had brought our drinks. "Why is my picture on the poster?"

Josh said, "While the champions play live pool here, they will also be showing shots from our place."

I asked, "How do I not know about all this?"

Josh said, "I told you I've blocked your feed on most things about the Big Hustles."

I said, "Maybe you should volunteer your services to the government to keep the Russians out of our elections."

He smiled, "Maybe I do."

Cam reached over and touched my arm, "Are you mad?"

"I don't understand? Why wouldn't you just tell me?"

Shannon said, "When things began, we thought they were little things, and we would save them to be surprises to share at the Hustle. Before we knew it, they had grown and become secrets. You seemed to have so much on your plate and then the assault. We're sorry, Perry."

I shook my head, "Maybe I understand, but don't protect me. All three of you know how that has been in my family. Any other secret surprises?"

Josh said, "There will be a member of the McDerman team at our event, and he will fill in for you so that you can take breaks, and you will play him last." I nodded okay. "Mr. McDerman is going to face time in at the end to thank you. Finally, as I said earlier, the AV team will be filming and editing to send out video highlights to the seven other centers and to post on YouTube. If there is other stuff, I don't know about it."

Our lunch came, and it was one of the best Reubens I ever had.

After she cleared our dishes, the waitress came back to the table and asked me, "Can the staff take a picture with you?"

I said, "Sure." With the bar in the background, they took a picture. Then our waitress handed me a Sharpie and asked if I would sign one of the posters advertising the event. I asked, "Why?"

"The boss thinks it will be a great silent auction item."

I said, "I doubt it." Right then every TV in the place lit up with Blotch vs. The Canary. The place was maybe a third full by now. Everyone turned from the screen to look at me. I waved. Cam grabbed my arm and whispered, "You're okay, right?"

I whispered back, "Yes." I was glad when it ended, but after the closing, there was film of a pool cue being slammed on a pool table and splintering. It just kept repeating. The minute it started Josh grabbed a chair and shoved it under me. Cam knelt in front of me, telling me to focus on her. I kept hearing it shatter and shatter and shatter and shatter ...

Shannon, unable to figure where the controls were, bellowed at the top of her lungs, "MAKE IT STOP, NOW!" All the screens went blank.

There was nothing but silence.

I felt someone holding my wrist and checking my pulse. She was pretty, maybe in her twenty's or thirty's. I asked, "Are you the nurse from the hospital?"

She said, "Yes, have you had panic attacks before?"

I didn't answer. My friends, who tell me nothing, volunteered, "He was mugged two weeks ago. The guy shattered his pool cue. They started then."

I said, "I'm okay." Someone gave me water to sip.

The nurse said, "I think you are. I'll be upstairs when you come back to see your granddad."

Cam and Shannon were still with me, Josh was on his phone. Someone, I assumed was the manager came to me and said, "We have played that tape, I don't know how many times, and it never ended like that."

I said, "There is someone who doesn't like me. It's okay."

Josh came back, "Demetri is going to take it down or crash that YouTube channel until they take it off. He says it's got the Mark of Cain all over it."

I said, "Josh, find that guy."

He said, "I will."

I stood, "Don't you get tired of taking care of me?" They claimed no, "Okay, I'm not going to let this guy ruin our day. Let's go see Philly." We took off to see the Liberty Bell and Independence Hall. I took a lot of pictures, and it was great. Josh surprised us all by singing

You see, we piddle, twiddle, and resolve
Not one damn thing do we solve
Piddle, twiddle, and resolve
Nothing's ever solved in
Foul, fetid, fuming, foggy, filthy
Philadephia!

It is a refrain from one of the songs from the musical 1776. Some of the other tourists watched and applauded.

We got back to the hospital at two. I called in, and the nurse from lunch came out and got me. She led me into the CCU, "They're with your granddad right now, but let's take your blood pressure and oxygen levels."

I said, "I'm fine. We've been out walking around."

She said, "I'm sure you are, but you're the most famous visitor we've had in the five years I've been on staff here."

"How am I famous?"

She laughed, "Tickets to your event at that restaurant have been sold out for a week."

I said, "I won't even be there."

"Everything seems to check out, and I think your granddad is ready now."

I went into Pop's room and hugged Nanna. They had moved Pop to one side of his bed along with all his wires and tubes. I took off my shoes and climbed into bed beside him. I was safe. I was asleep in minutes.

Cam was in the room when they woke me up. I kissed Pops on the cheek. I said, "I like your Blotch bruise; you get better."

He said, "I am better, Perry."

I told him, "I'm coming back for a week this summer."

Pops said, "I'll hold you to that."

Cam kissed Pops on the cheek, we both kissed Nanna. Josh and Shannon had gone down to the lobby to get us a cab. My nap made us pushed for time.

Homeward Bound

We caught our train fine and were settled in heading home. We were quiet. I thought, 'I want to marry Cam when I'm eighteen and have kids right away. I want our children to know Pops and Nanna and Mr. and Mrs. Grant. If I'm supposed to get a masters or a doctorate in something I can do that later. I think I'll take care of the kids and let Cam get all the education.' Is it too soon to tell Cam my plans? Would it scare her off?

She caught me smiling. "What are you smiling about?"

"I'm just smiling."

We again had facing seats. Suddenly Josh shouted, "Short bells!"

Shannon said, "Short what?"

A woman sitting across the aisle gave Josh a very adult look. Cam asked the woman, "Did you hear 'Bells?'"

She said, "I did not."

Josh blushed and to her said, "I said 'Bells, Bells.'"

The lady laughed, "You're cute when you blush." She turned back to her book.

Josh said to us, "She said I was cute."

Cam laughed, "It didn't sound like bells."

He continued, "Anyway there have been two or three times the trolling came outside of fourth period, and that was because those days had short bells." It means the class schedule for the day was adjusted to fit an assembly or early dismissal. "All the trolling has been fourth period by someone who doesn't have to sign in to use the computer. Perry, I'll know by lunch tomorrow. I promise you."

I smiled, "You are the best. I hope you are protecting us from those Russians. When are you going to unblock all my channels?"

He laughed, "Soon."

My phone rang. It was Mom, "Hi Mom, how was your retreat?"

Me: I'm glad to hear it. Listen I need to tell you some things. I want you to find a safe place to pull off the road and call me back. Just do as I ask, yes I'm okay. Call me back.

I hung up. Five minutes later they called back.

Mom and Dad on speaker: Young man you better have a good reason why you are in Pennsylvania. You were told not to leave the state without permission. You need to start talking.

Remember, they have the same tracking app Cam has.

Me: Are you stopped and in a safe place?

Mom and Dad: Yes, but we are far more concerned about where you are.

Me: Pops had a heart attack.

I just let that lay there for a moment.

Me: Pop was asking for me, and the Bentons and Nanna decided I could go up on the train today. Josh, Cam, and Shannon came with me.

Mom and Dad: We're so sorry Perry. We should have listened first. We're glad you went. Are you okay?

Me: I'm good. The heart attack was mild. They put some things in to hold his arteries open.

Mom and Dad: Perry, we are so sorry. Look we're going to call Nanna. If we head to Philly, do you think you could stay with the Bentons a few more days?

Me: I'm sure that will be okay. Just so you know, I missed you.

Mom and Dad: Perry, we love you.

We were facing each other, Josh and I across from each other, the girls asleep beside us. I was answering texts on my phone. Josh kicked my foot, "Remember what you said at the restaurant about how much trouble you are?"

I remembered, "Yeah."

"Well, you are the most high maintenance guy I've ever known or known about."

I frowned, "Thanks?"

He chuckled, "Well, here's the thing. I sat with some guys before I came to sit with you and Cam. When I quit sitting with them, they never came and looked for me. When we talked, they never said come back and sit with us. I know you would look for me. Then you got me together with Shannon. There is more college essay material in working on the Big Hustle than anyone imagined. I can't imagine what the next three years of high school hold for us. And I think Rick is right about Blotch power. I used to be nervous to tell people I had made a revolutionary war video game or that I liked comics. Now I tell people who I am and it doesn't affect me what they think. I feel better about myself, I'm proud of who I am. The benefits go on and on, but here's the bottom line, you're my brother."

"You know I'm not really your brother?"

He said, "I know one day we'll do those DNA tests and I'll be right, and you'll be wrong. I think we are descended from the Denisovans, though I see a lot of Neanderthal in you. Anyway, I'll always be here for you."

The rest of the trip was quiet. Mr. Benton picked us all up. Cam's father had something for me, so I was going to her house, Josh was going to get his car and take Shannon home.

When we got to Cam's, Mr. Grant had posters from the six other venues hosting fundraisers. I asked, "How can these already be here and why here?"

Mr. Grant laughed, "Cam told me they were reading you in on more. I helped Cam make contact with Mr. McDerman. He and I realized we met about six years ago at a Kiwanis International Convention. Anyway, I guess around noon you signed a poster in Philly, and they posted a picture. Well, the events coordinator saw it, she got in touch with me, and sent poster files to Staples. I picked them up at four."

I said, "That makes my head spin. I think it is ridiculous to think anyone is going to pay money for a poster signed by Blotch." I sat down and signed each of the posters.

Then Mr. Grant pulled out a package, "And this came for you."

I knew it was my cue. My hands shook as I opened it. Instead of the plastic case, I now had a solid case with a felt inside formed to fit the cue. It was beautiful. I was ridiculously happy to have it back. I put it together and ran my hand all over it.

I kissed Cam good night and headed home to Josh's.

I made myself a sandwich and headed back to our room. I didn't even finish my sandwich before I lay back on my bed and fell asleep holding my pool cue. Did I tell you they got me a real bed for our birthday to replace the inflatable bed? My bed felt so good.

Not All Trolls Live Under Bridges

At lunch, Josh said, "Follow me." We sat down at a table across from Waylon and Roger. Josh said, "Waylon is the troll."

"Why Waylon?"

"Because I can't stand you."

I was amazed, "I don't think we've ever spoken."

He was getting mad, "Here is how I see it. You're ugly, and nobody cares. I have to wear an ankle brace that affects how I walk, and sometimes I stutter, and I'm constantly ridiculed."

When he said ugly, I reached over and touched Josh's arm because he was ready to go all Cam on Waylon. "That sucks Waylon, and yes, I'm Blotched, and I'm ugly."

Waylon was still mad, "Well the guy in the park said the Mark of Cain thing would mess with you. I didn't even know what it meant when I started."

I closed my eyes and sighed, "The guy in the park? The guy with the dog?" he nodded. "You didn't know I had a twin who died before we were born?"

He said, "No man, how would I know that?"

I asked, "How about the pool cue thing?"

He laughed, and then he stuttered a little, (I'm not going to try to write his stutter. I think that would be rude.) "I came up with that on my own after the mall attack."

I put a firmer grip on Josh's arm, "What do you want Waylon?"

"I want what you have, respect."

I kept my grip on Josh, who was not happy, "Then come join our table; come work on the Hustle. You can obviously do videos; you can join Josh's AV team. He needs all the help he can get on Saturday."

"Just go. I won't troll you anymore, but I don't want any of what you have to hand out."

"It's an open offer. Come for it when you're ready."

He waved us off with his middle finger. Josh and I headed back to our lunch group. Josh couldn't believe I let it go down like that. I assured him Waylon would be there to help out on Saturday, and I told him he better treat him with respect. Waylon showed up at our table just before the bell, "I'll help with the AV stuff Saturday, What time?"

Josh politely said, "See you at the restaurant at eleven."

I said, "Waylon, see you at lunch tomorrow."

He said, "Not happening."

I told him, "You can sit with me, or I'll sit with you."

I tried to explain to the table that this was reconciliation through non-violence. While they could see it, they had a hard time getting over their resentment about what Waylon had done to me. I try hard to show them that resentment does nothing but breed negativity within themselves. I think I'm making some progress. I finally explained to them, "Waylon had a real dislike for me, but he was a pawn of the man in the park. And for whatever reason, the man in the park thought I needed to know about my brother who died." Everyone knew about the mysterious man, but only Josh, Shannon, and

Cam knew the whole story and knew he was an angel.
No one asked how the man in the park could know
about my brother.

The Big Hustle

Joshn stayerd over at my house the night beore the Hustle. That morning I was a nervous wreck. Josh was too. We got short with each other. I yelled at him, "You need to make less noise; you're making me nervous!" Josh yelled back, "All you have to do is play pool and go around once an hour being nice to people. I've got a team of five guys making movies, including Waylon, thank you very much. I have four cameramen, and I have to condense every hour of you playing pool into shorts with titles."

When he quit shouting, we just stood in our room staring at each, and then we cracked up. I said, "Our first fight."

We kept laughing until we cried.

We met up with everyone else at the restaurant at ten-thirty. Josh was working audiovisual. Ashtyn, Sean, and Letty, now his girlfriend, were working the front door seating people. Rick was going to be commentating some and also interviewing various people. There were TVs all over the walls. You could choose to watch the pool table, watch Rick, or watch the shorts as Josh put them out. Each table had a small speaker so you could listen to what you chose to watch. Cam, because she has the same name talent as I do, would work the room talking with people. Gene was lining up the people to play me. There were some scheduled games, but we decided to take people as they came. All we did was ask for a donation. They got back twice what they donated if they won.

Slider, Butch and some of their biker friends were there as security. Also, some off-duty police had volunteered to help, including Officer James and Officer JJ, who came down from Pennsylvania.

Dara from Monroe was the first girl I would play. She didn't have to make a donation, but she put up fifty. She smiled as she said, "I think fifty and a kiss is going to make this a very sweet afternoon."

Cam had said the only rule was they couldn't touch me unless they won the kiss.

Dara's strategy was to distract me with math challenges. As I set up my shot she asked:

"What's the square root of 9,723?"

"98.605."

"What's the next to the last digit if you take Pi out fourteen decimal points?"

"Seven."

"What is the significance of 1.48.54.01.40?"

"Well, that is the traditional translation of the first column of line six of tablet P322 if that is what you are looking for."

Rick had Roger, Waylon's friend helping him, who immediately googled P322, so Rick was able to add, "P322 is a 3500-year-old Babylonian clay tablet believed by some to be the first evidence of trigonometry."

"What is the last digit of seven to the seventy-seventh."

"Seven."

"One train leaves from Los Angeles at 78 miles per hour. Another train leaves from New York two and a half hours later traveling 88 miles per hour. The total distance from city to city is 2800 miles. Which train is closest to New York when they meet?"

"Oh, I like you. That is tricky. There are just enough details to make you think it's a math question. Even right now math nerds are trying to figure out the equation, and non-math nerds are thinking, 'I hate word problems,' but this is a logic question. When they meet, they are at the same distance."

By sinking most of her balls for her, she lost by only one ball. I let her kiss me on the cheek.

I alternated letting people lose by one or two balls and just clearing the table. A boy who looked ten or eleven and had no hair came up to play. He had a cute smile, but dark and sunken eyes. A look I had left the hospital with on more than one occasion. As we were getting ready to start, Ashtyn came and whispered in my ear. "Slider says, right here, right now, we are about to find out if you are a human genius or only a math nerd."

I looked around the room for Slider. He waved to me. I looked back at the boy. I asked, "What's your name?"

He said, "Quentin."

I said, "Hi Quentin, my name is Perry, but everyone calls me Blotch. Have you missed much school this year?"

He said, "I have my own tutor, but I miss my friends."

I said, "When I was your age I was homeschooled, and I didn't have but one or two friends. It was a bummer. You ready to play some pool?"

I helped him win, leaving me with four balls on the table. The room erupted in applause. I told him, "One of the rules is you get the money, but you may not have known the other rule is you give me a hug." After we hugged, his parents wanted pictures. Seeing I was setting him up to win, Josh had printed off an, I beat the BLOTCH certificate. I signed it, and they took him out on camera for Rick to present it. When the video showed at the seven other venues, they also erupted in applause. Like me, everyone was certain Quentin must be very sick.

After all that, I took my first break. Rudy from the McDerman team took over for me. Cam and I went around to each table. If there was a student we knew, we could quickly name the rest of the family. We thanked people for coming. We thanked people who had volunteered or contributed. There were a number of kids on the spectrum. They mostly had on sound-deadening earphones.

After my break, I was to play Shane from Thomlinson. Four cheerleaders from her school had come with her. They ran around the restaurant shouting cheers and then went out on camera with Rick. The stage was set up out in the mall with the silent auction. The bands were also playing out in the mall. They did another round of cheers before he interviewed them.

They each had a family member who was on the spectrum.

Shane started by kissing a stripe and then a solid ball, "I kissed them for luck. Are you lucky?"

Okay I blushed, I didn't want to, but I did, "I think I'm more skilled than lucky."

The crowd was reading all kind of things into this. She shot first and had a nice break. Sank one and missed her next shot. When I went to shoot, she leaned over and breathed on my ear. I sank my shot. Before my next shot, she kissed the tip of her pool cue. The crowd loved her. I focused as best I could and started sinking balls. I needed this to wrap up sooner rather than later. As I was clearing the table, she started pouting.

"Are you in a hurry for me to leave?"

"Only because I don't know what will happen if you stay a minute longer." I sank the eight ball. She gave me a kiss on the cheek.

The Congressman was on the schedule next, but he was late, so I kept taking all comers. I had talked to the treasurer earlier and decided he was innocent. I hoped the Congressman was bringing good news. When he arrived, Sean escorted him and his aide over. The local news magazine had shown up, but they weren't allowed to take photos. They would be given copies from our camera people.

I let the Congressman break, he sank a solid. He sank a second ball and then missed, "You're not going to clear the table and embarrass me?"

I lined up my shot, "Did you bring me good news?"

He patted his coat pocket, "I have a grant check right here for twenty-five thousand dollars. Somehow it got lost."

I sank one and missed my next on purpose, "So after we play, we'd like Sean to take you around and introduce you to some of the key volunteers. These students have done an amazing thing in just six weeks."

He sank one and missed one.

As I lined up my next shot, I said "After that we'd like you to go up on stage with Rick and present the check and tell the students what a fabulous job they have done. How impressed you are?"

He sank another one, "And you, what you have done."

Smiling I said, "Here's the deal you have to agree to, or I'll sweep the table. Okay?" I sank one, "You can say how much fun it was to play me, but you don't give any credit to me. I want the message today to focus on the over sixty student volunteers who have had a powerful positive impact on our community. I don't want it about me. Agreed?"

He shook his head, "Slider told me you saw the world differently. I agree."

I sank one of mine and accidentally two of his. I missed my next shot and left him a perfect line up on his last ball. He sank it but missed the eight ball shot. I cleared my balls and sank the eight. We shook, and our guys took photos. He did as I asked, and Ms. Patel and the treasurer were there to accept the check.

Josh asked if anyone on the AV team wanted to go on camera and be interviewed by Rick. Waylon jumped up, "I just finished a film. I'll go."

Josh was not smiling, "Are you sure, Waylon?"

Waylon laughed, "I won't mess it up."

Josh was still not happy, he told him, "The rule is nothing good or bad about Perry, or we pull the audio feed."

Waylon bounced out of the room.

Rick: Hi Waylon, what are you working on?

Waylon: Actually, I'm making your interviews into short films to be posted.

Rick: How do I look on camera?

Waylon: The camera loves you, Rick.

Rick gave Josh a look. I know they were both wondering what happened to the angry Waylon. Waylon took the pause as a chance to control the interview.

Waylon: I guess you want to know how I came to volunteer for the Big Hustle.

Rick: Yeah, that was my next question.

Waylon: From the beginning I had a bug up my butt about this whole thing, everybody so happy and positive. I wear an ankle brace that makes me walk funny, and sometimes I stutter. Generally, I'm not a very happy guy, and I didn't like so many happy people. Especially the Josh guy who is running AV.

Rick: Josh?

Waylon: Especially him. I started trolling him. It took him over four weeks to figure out it was me. I actually thought he was more computer savvy than that.

So Monday he shows up at my lunch table. You know what the amazing thing was?

Rick: No, what?

Waylon: He wasn't angry or anything. He just said, 'What's up Waylon?' I told him, 'I don't like you.' He comes back with 'I don't always like myself. Do you want to come help on the Big Hustle AV team on Saturday?' At first, I told him no, but really I did want to help, and I'm glad he asked me and glad he let me.

Rick: Wow, Waylon! What a story. Any last words?

Waylon laughing: It felt so good to get that bug out of my butt. And what I learned here was if the way I walk or when I stutter bothers you, too bad. This is just who Waylon is.

When he came down, Josh asked, "What was that all about?"

Waylon said, "I decided I like you."

Josh was undone.

After Waylon finished, Sean and Gene went up for an interview.

Gene: Maybe some of you have seen the video of me being a jerk to Sean. Only about a million people saw it, so maybe you missed it. (Everyone laughed) When my brother saw it, he told me I was a jerk and told me I needed to sit down and talk to Sean. My brother was right; I was choosing to be a jerk.

Sean: I was nervous about sitting down with Gene, but it took place in the school cafeteria during lunch, just four students at a table. The principal and other adults were standing close by. I'm glad I did it.

Gene: I have chosen to stop being a jerk. We now eat lunch together every day. And tonight after the Hustle, we're taking our girlfriends out on a double date.

Sean: We are?

Gene: Don't you ever check your messages?

They walked off together.

Nicholas made an appearance to talk about the spectrum club. He also had family there from out of town, and his cousin on the spectrum was there. Karalyne and Serena talked about the auction. Rick also interviewed each of the bands before they went up to play. My parents arrived for my four o'clock break. Josh had a computer set up in Mr. Jakes office tied into an Ethernet line. He explained the wireless was overloaded. I didn't know what this was about. I sat down in front of the screen and Josh clicked it open. There was Pops.

Me: Pops, where are you?

Pops: I'm at the sports bar by the hospital.

Me: Why?

Pops: They sent a car for Nanna and me, so we could see you play. You're doing a great job.

Me: Thanks Pops, how did this happen?

Pops: I think a nurse from the hospital set it up. They're treating us like we're famous, and we're having a great time. You keep up the good work.

Me: Love you Pops.

I was so happy I was ready to cry. I hugged Mom and Dad and then Cam. We went out to do a quick affirmation tour of the silent auction. Did I tell you it had to be set up in the mall because there wasn't enough room in the restaurant for everything the girls had gotten? What I am seeing is how much is possible when we work together.

I had a talk with Henry this past week. I told him I didn't feel I had done all that much to make this happen, and that I was shaping the message to be about what an amazing thing all these teenagers had come together to do. He agreed, but he also insisted that it would not have happened without me. I am still not sure about that.

Close to the End

I was getting a little tired, so we had stretched our break until four-fifteen. Karalyne was waiting at the table to play me. I had seen her earlier, and her outfit was unremarkable. Maybe a little too much for school but not by much. However now she had changed a few things. There was so little of it left; I'll take the time to describe it. On her legs, she had a style of jeans that hugged every curve of her body from her ankles until four or more inches below her belly button. Believe me, I wasn't getting close enough to measure. Earlier she had on a long tail shirt and a leather vest. The shirt was gone. The vest had a gap up the center laced together by a small gold chain going from button hole to button hole. You could see skin all the way up from her navel to her neck. A fob at the bottom of the chain rested on her belly button.

Cam was standing at the table. She had her fingernail board out working on her nails as though all was okay. I asked, "Is this okay?"

Cam didn't even look up, "I said as far as I was concerned the only rule was they couldn't touch you unless they won the kiss. She's not touching you is she?"

I said, "No."

She asked, "Do you have feelings for Karalyne?"

I said, "No."

Cam said, "Then I don't see it matters what she wears."

I started counting backward from a hundred in Spanish.

Cam still doing her nails said, "Perry, if you are having lusty thoughts, that is not Karalyne's fault. Perry, are you having lusty thoughts?"

I lied, "No." I continued counting in Spanish.

I let Karalyne break. Nothing sank. I sank one of mine. On my second shot, I deliberately sank one of hers and one of mine. I missed my third shot. She had a way of sliding her hand up and down her pool cue that kept me focused on counting in Spanish.

She sank one and was so happy. She exclaimed with glee, "I've snatched two balls." (Yes, she exclaimed it with glee.)

I was shooting diagonally across the table. She was standing right at the spot toward which I was aiming. With precision timing, just as my cue started moving, she bent down to pick up something off the floor. Only her tightly wrapped bottom stood above the edge of the table. I lost it. The cue ball became airborne, bounced on her bottom, and off into the crowd.

She rose up with a smile on her face, "Why Perry, I felt that little scratch." (Scratch, actually is the term for the ball leaving the table.)

I dropped my cue on the table and said, "I forfeit."

She jumped up and down, clapped her hands together and ran around the table to me. She leaned in for the kiss. It was gentle and nice, and I forgot myself and kissed a little too long. Every TV screen in the restaurant was showing a close up of our kiss, there is a slight delay, so it was still going on as we separated. The cameras cut to Cam. I turned to her. She yelled, "I said you could kiss them, but you weren't supposed to enjoy it!" She turned her back to me but didn't run away. Then she doubled over. I thought she was sick. When she came back up, she turned toward me, and broke into laughter so hard she started crying. Then Karalyne and the whole room was laughing.

As the crowd calmed down, Rick came on the screen, "Perry, the girls planned all this. Cam helped Karalyne with her outfit and her ... a ... performance. Perry, you have been had." I went over and kissed Cam. When the screen went back to Rick, he said, "What you guys who date girls put up with?" The room went silent. Roger came into camera view. He whispered in Rick's ear. Rick turned bright red, and looked down, composing himself. He came back up looking at the camera and half sung, half spoke;

Hello Muddahs
Hello Faddahs
Hello Bruddahs
Hello Sistahs
Did I tell yahs
I like the Fellahs.

The room erupted in standing applause. Apparently, all seven other locations, who had tuned in for the kiss, did also. There is a big difference between coming out to your friends and family versus announcing it in a live broadcast to maybe thousands of strangers. (We are almost to the end, and I wish there would be a way to tell you everything that happened because of the Big Hustle and about the other things we would do in high school. But I want you to know this moment, more than anything else is what got Rick an internship at a TV station.)

I only had a few more games before my five o'clock break which I took early. Rudy took over which was fine because he did a lot of entertaining trick shots and was a great showman. The people loved him. Josh and Cam were there to take me back to Mr. Jake's office. A minor headliner from one of the cable channels had shown up and wanted to interview me. Here is the gist of how it went.

I went in and sat down across from him. I said, "This is totally off the record. You can't quote me, talk about me, or use my name without my permission; I'm a minor." He nodded okay. "You think you want this story about this boy who rose above his Blotch and did something wonderful for the Renaissance Center. That's not the story. You can, however, say the story is that over sixty high school students stepped forward and volunteered themselves to help raise an amazing amount of money. They learned, they grew, and they took risks. Each of them has a great story of what they did, what they learned, and why they did it. Josh can put together a series of Rick's interviews with some of them. You can put yourself on with a lead-in and closing. It's a big and powerful story."

Thankfully, he agreed. We shook and said goodbye. Josh stayed with him to discuss the details and maybe to try to explain me.

Cam and I started our table visits. Mrs. Pennington and her husband along with little Bethany from the milk cooler were in a booth. Bethany scrambled to stand up on the seat and raised her arms to me. I don't know if it was okay or not, but I picked her up. As she had before, she shoved my face to the right and kissed Blotch. She pulled away and said, "Blessing."

Cam asked, "Do all the girls want to kiss you?"

Mr. and Mrs. Pennington were standing now. Mrs. Pennington leaned in and kissed me on my right cheek and said, "I think they do."

I shook hands with Mr. Pennington, and they took a lot of pictures. As we walked away, I asked Cam, "You're not really jealous are you?"

She turned and faced me. She put her arms around my neck and said, "I think someday you're going to make a great dad." She leaned in and kissed me. Cell phone cameras were going wild around us.

Rudy, the McDerman champ, and I played the last game at five-thirty. He was way better than me and, with his help, he only beat me by one ball. We were now at the final wrap up. Mr. McDerman came on the TV screens. "Perry, I would like to thank you for what you have done for your local center and for inspiring us to host seven additional hustles across the country. In addition to what you have done, those seven hustles that were inspired by your team have raised a combined total of over a hundred thousand dollars to support centers in their communities. Also while you have had a rather busy day, a team of professionals and volunteers have put a new roof on the Renaissance Center and repaired all the interior water damage." The room applauded. "Now before I go, I want you to meet my nephew, John."

John wasn't looking at the camera, but he said, "Thank you, Perry." Then he said it in sign language with Marlin's signs for U Blotch R.

Rick came on and started reading through the totals raised, "Our fundraising is a cooperation, not a competition, but the low man in that cooperation is Perry playing pool at $2,620. Perry, you might want to start looking for a real job." Everyone laughed. "Raised by reservations, meals, and donations from the wait staff, $5,200. Raised by the silent auction $8,925. Thank you shopping girls. Raised from sponsors primarily recruited by the Spectrum Club, $39,000; altogether putting us well over our goal of forty thousand." The room broke into wild applause. When they quieted down, a drum roll started. Rick came back on. "Before I announce our Fundsup page I want to share this from the Young Entrepreneurs Conference in Richmond. The video entries our guys and girls did got a third in all videos, and one got a first in its category." Again applause. "Now, our Fundsup page. We asked Quentin's parents if we could put him beating Blotch up. They not only agreed; they insisted. In the hour after it went up, we received $15,000 in donations, which makes him our second biggest fundraiser after Pah and Marlin whose films, along with additional videos our AV team has put up today, has passed $79,000 and is still climbing."

The TV guy came up to me. He said, "You're right. They are the bigger story, but I hope if you ever want to share your story, you will give me first crack at it." He gave me his card and walked away.

Rick, Cam, Josh and I all knew what was coming and we were two minutes early. Rick went into some thank yous to the bands, announced that the Mall had said the ShadowMan Band could play until eight. Apparently, it had almost been like Christmas sales at the mall. Rick stopped talking as almost every phone in the room beeped. Josh had hacked into the school phone system to send out a text to every parent, student, teacher, and administrator. 'What you have done is amazing. I hope you are proud of your accomplishments, and please know we are truly thankful.' Anonymous. That was followed thirty seconds later by a personal thank you from me to each of the volunteers.

The crowd turned to me. Following Rick, who was on the screen, they said in sign language, 'Thank You, U Blotch R.'

I Could Have Danced All Night

The restaurant emptied out. They planned to clear the place and reopen at seven thirty. All our people were packing out their stuff. I gave Mom and Dad my cue to take home. Alone, except for the restaurant staff, our group plopped down at a table. None of us could believe what we had done. I hoped the angel man from the park was happy. I wondered why he cared so much.

The band must have been playing a thunderous song because we could hear them. Cam said, "I wish we could go dance."

I asked, "Why can't we?"

Shannon said, "There is another film crew out there. They are trying to scoop the one you turned down. It would be better if we just went to the coffee shop or home."

Josh said, "Henry closed the coffee shop tonight, and I want to take my girl dancing."

I said, "Ashtyn, call up Operation Blotch."

Josh and I had seen this possibility, and with Ashtyn's help had set up a plan. Ashtyn was very close to some of the students in the drama department, and right then four of them came rolling in on those skate shoes. (They are a fad that comes around every so often. You click them, and the wheels pop out. You click again, and the wheels go away.)

It was quite a sight. Kermit's head is mostly shaved except for a purple ponytail, Shandle has cornrows, Tim has bright red hair, and Tara has no hair. (I know I don't usually talk about hair, but I thought you would want to know.)

Kermit skated right up beside Cam and me and unrolled a make-up kit. Cam jumped up, I stood up. Cam said, with a voice just short of shouting, "If you are going to let him paint over Blotch, and then you think I would dance with you, well that is not happening."

I said, "Now, Cam, listen."

She was not calming down, she was getting louder, "I don't need to listen to anything. Haven't we been through enough? I thought it was decided U Blotch R." (She made the sign as she spoke.)

I said, "Yes."

Cam paused long enough for Kermit to ask, "Are you ready Cam?"

She turned toward him practically yelling, "No, I'm not ready if he is going to let you paint over Blotch I'm leaving. I'm with Rick, this has been about being empowered to be yourself."

Kermit said, "Yes."

She paused long enough to see that everyone was being painted with a Blotch. Shandle was just finishing painting on Josh's Blotch.

Cam transformed, "Yes, I'm ready." She sat down.

All Blotched, we headed out into the Mall. As we left the restaurant, Bethany ran up to me shouting, "Blessing!"

I picked her up and kissed her on her Blotch mark and then turned so she could kiss mine. Mr. and Mrs. Pennington had followed close behind. Mrs. Pennington said, "She wouldn't leave until you had seen her blessing mark."

As we started dancing, I realized people were wearing nametags. Most of them said I am Blotch, but I realized others said, "I'm Gay, I'm Blonde," Four-foot-nine Cindy's said, "I'm Short." Rick had been right. For many people, the Big Hustle had been an empowerment to say, "See me. I am who I am." Waylon, who had come a long way, had a slightly different take on the message. His said, "I S-T-U-T-T-E-R FU." How Waylon to add, "FU." He clearly meant if it bothers you, that's your problem. Some said things that concerned me and, while I danced with all my heart, I tried to remember them. One said, "I'm scared" and another said, "I'm lonely."

The film crews finally gave up on finding Blotch and left. The ShadowMan band played:

I'm a Blotchy boy in a Blotchy world
Don't know how I ever found a girl.
I could dance all night, You are my light,
Please let me hold you tight,
I'm a Blotchy boy in a Blotchy world.
Don't know how I ever found a girl.

It was a take-off from a song, "I'm a Barbie Girl." Cam wouldn't stop laughing as I turned bright red. When they sang it again, I joined in. The third time the whole dance floor was singing.

We were close to eight o'clock and the last song of the evening. A buzz started moving through the crowd.

Cam told me, "Henry made it back from the meeting in Richmond."

My answer was an uninspired, "That's nice." But as I looked around the room I could see that all the dancers lights were an excited anticipation.

Cam told me, "You don't understand. He's going to sit in on the last song."

No, I didn't understand. I didn't know that because of what was about to happen the ShadowBand, if accompanied by Henry, was not allowed to play at school dances. I said, "That's nice."

"Wait, you'll see."

I had wondered why there were two drum sets on the stage. For the most part, the Bands had shared one drum set and amps. Henry went up and sat at the extra set joining Terry the ShadowMan Band drummer.

The band started a new number beginning with just the lead guitar. It was the kind of slow number where you hold each other close and move slowly to the music. The second guitar and the bass joined in. The tune was familiar, but maybe it had no words. Terry came in on the drums. They started over. Henry came in. I'm not sure whether to try to describe the music or what it did to me. The auras of all the dancers slowly moved from warmth to passion. Henry played a rhythm in and around and opposite of what the band played. I felt the passion and warmth in my body. I closed my eyes so I only thought of Cam and me. My body, our bodies continued to move with the music of the band, but my heart, my soul, our hearts, our souls rode through the heavens on the rhythm of the music of the angels. I could no longer hold back. I could no longer contain my feelings. I whispered in her ear, "I'm going to marry you." She whispered back, "……"

Some Questions

1. Why do you think Cam enjoys playing tricks on Perry? (Like hiding in the mall bathroom and helping Karalyne play him in pool.)
2. Why do you think the author chose Rick to get Perry to come out of seclusion? If you had to choose another character to take Rick's spot who would you choose? Why?
3. What makes Perry climb into his Pop's hospital bed? Do you think he does it for Pops or for himself?
4. What is the significance of Perry turning his face to the left? What is he feeling when he does this?
5. Do you think it is possible for a friend to become a "real" sister or brother? Why or Why not?
6. When you are feeling at your worst who do you turn to for help? What qualities do/does that person/people have that makes you turn to them?
7. Why is it important in life to be okay with who you are?
8. Do you think Perry should have taken more credit for the Big Hustle? Why or why not?
9. How does being anonymous empower some people to bully others?
10. Do you think Perry's parents were justified to keep the death of his twin a secret from him? Why or why not?
11. Choose a minor character who you think influences the story the most. Why do you think he or she has such a powerful influence?

12. If you were the author and had to choose someone other than Perry to be the main character of Blotch 4 who would you chose and why?
13. If you attended the dance at the Big Hustle what would you put on your nametag? Why?
14. When Perry tells Cam he wants to marry her, what do you think she says?

Acknowledgments

My thanks to those who read and edited this story as it developed, especially Michel Schadt, Vinnie Lainson, and Rachel Strohman. Many of the minor characters are named after youth who I have discussed the story and particular scenes with. I read two to three MG and YA books a week, and I am thankful to the many authors who delight and inspire me.

Rick's song, "Hello Muddahs, Hello Faddahs" is a takeoff on the opening lines of "Camp Granada," by Allan Sherman.

The song "Barbie Girl" is by Aqua.

In some ways, the story did not correspond to the Virginia driving laws. You must be 16 years and three months to get a license. A new driver under 18 can only carry 1 other passenger under the age of 18.

Stuart is known as a storyteller and entertaining speaker. He loves to test his story ideas with his audience. Stuart lives and writes at his home, Greenway Cottage, on the edge of the Virginia Piedmont.

Youth Advisors

Aidan	Frank	Trent
Amanda	Olivia	Zach
Colin	Serena	
Carolyn	Shannon	

All characters were defined before the assignment of names and the characters in no way reflect the individuals whose names were used.

Other Books by Stuart

Henry on Fire

Henry and the ShadowMan Band

Henry in Stand with Fred Friday

Mom, Dad, I Killed a Man

Tales of the Mountain Boy and other stories

Blotch in the Mirror (Book One)

Pray the Angels Come Back (Blotch Book Two)

www.ingramcontent.com/pod-product-compliance
Lightning Source LLC
Chambersburg PA
CBHW030257130626
46549CB00002B/573